Searching
for
Carolina

Jade Heffington

To Mrs Ward! Thanks for everything! ♡

Jade Heffington

ISBN: 172786204X
ISBN-13: 978-1727862041

Searching for Carolina

3

CONTENTS

THIS IS LONDON.

This is it. England.

The train ride to our campus was long. The plane ride, even more so. But here we are. Finally, I get to explore the streets of London.

If it wasn't for my college class, I would have never gotten this opportunity. For two reasons. One, I don't have nearly enough money for the trip and two, I'm still in high school. I wouldn't be able to take this much time off unless it was for another class. Then and only then would I be excused.

I felt someone tapping my shoulder, pulling me out of my thoughts. When I turn around I see that it is just one of my classmates. I still have yet to remember any of their names. Since I spend more than half the day in my hometown at the high school, I don't get the chance to see these people all the time like they see each other. She points to her ear and then in front of her. My eyes follow her gaze and I see our instructor standing at the front of the bus.

I quickly unplug my earphones and try to pay attention to what's left of the instructions. But once I start hearing what the balding, middle aged man in front of us was actually saying, I started to daydream. He's just repeating himself again anyway. Nothing I haven't heard a million and one times on this trip already, and I bet I'll hear them again.

'Stick together... don't wander off without your roommates or a buddy... always keep your dorm room keys on you... blah blah blah.'

We aren't five. We're in college. Except for me, obviously, but if I'm mature enough to take a college class then I'm mature enough to follow directions without someone having to repeat them every few minutes.

"Alright class. You have tonight to get settled and then we have an early morning." I think when he said early morning, every single teen on the bus started to groan. Maybe even the driver. Everyone, that is, except for me. I'm more of a morning person and I can't wait to get started on this project. I just don't know what part of England's history I want to dive into.

As we step off the bus and into the college dorm lobby, Professor Gates hands us all a map and a list of places to gather research. He took the time to create a list of every library within walking radius. Surprisingly, there are quite a few.

"These are your guides and your maps. I advise you to keep them with you every place you go. Along with your keys and roommates, of course." Professor Gates is the only one laughing. Everyone else is just standing there with blank expressions waiting for the moment they finally get to be away from him. I don't have anything against our instructor, and being here in London is absolutely mind boggling so I'm thankful for that, but I think we're all pretty exhausted from the flight.

"Well, I won't keep you here any longer. Head off to your rooms. But remember, I will be having late night pop-ins to make sure everything's in order. We don't want anyone interrupting other residents now, do we?" Again, he's the only one laughing.

As the handful of students start to head up the stairs all trying to drag along beside them their luggage, I decide to wait at the bottom of the stairway. There's no way I'm going to be corralled up what, five flights of stairs? I'm liable to fall backwards taking at least one of these people with me. That wouldn't be the best way to start off this trip.

As I lay my suitcase longways to make a chair for myself, I take out my phone. I don't know what time it would be back home, but I do know my mother wanted me to call her when we landed. Which I didn't do. What is the time difference between Tennessee and London? Currently in London it's about eight. I'll just call her in the morning. I'm glad my phone clock changes for me. I don't even know how to work it, honestly. I'm not a tech savvy person. I'm more old fashioned. I'm probably worse than my parents. I just recently got this phone from them because we could never afford one. The day I brought home my permission slip was the day they started to scrap and save up. They wanted me to be able to talk to them whenever I wanted, and to be able to always have a way to call for help. Now, I have all that and more at my fingertips. I just figured out the text messaging on this thing and it's great. I mean, it gets complicated sometimes, but once you get the hang of it having a cell phone is pretty nifty.

I raise my head and see that the herd of teens has finally disappeared from my view. I guess that's my cue to head upstairs. I get up off my bag and start dragging it upward thinking, 'why don't they have an elevator?'.

Five floors, a couple burning thighs, a puddle of sweat and about fifty cramps later, I finally reach my room. I dig out my key from my pocket and unlock the door. I don't exactly know who my roommate is yet. Professor Gates just handed out keys. Randomly. I wonder if he even put any thought into it. Meaning, did he make the rooms gender-neutral or separated the way they should be.

Struggling to hold the door open as I enter with my luggage and jello-like legs, I walk around the corner and find nothing other than what I sort of expected myself: a boy. His personal items are already laid out on his desk and his body is spread across his horrifically made bed reading a book. When he notices me his head jolts up and a smile forms on his face.

"I knew I was gonna get a gal…" he says while shaking his head and returning to what I could only make out to be an old history book. I guess he's decided to start early. Even before we go sightseeing tomorrow.

Walking over to my side of the room I notice he had brought along his guitar. Good. There's one positive thing about this roommate. He's a musician. I sing a little myself. Not really to anyone but my family, friends and my church, but still.

As I start unpacking my things I hear the boy on the other side of the room start to hum. I didn't know he sang also. That tune sounds familiar.

"You listen to *Paper Lions*?" I turn back around when he asks that question. It was until then I realise that I had been humming along with him. As a shy smile found its way onto my face along with the blush rising to my cheeks, I gave him a small nod. I watch him as he closes the book and flings his feet over the side of the bed. He starts to stare at me while slowly getting closer. I quickly move backwards until the back of my knees hit the side of my bed, as if it were a reflex. But instead of doing any of the unsettling acts I thought he was going to, he surprises me when he holds out his free hand in front of me.

"Since we're basically partners, I'm Rian." He stands there waiting for my hand to meet his, but for some reason it never does.

I look down to his hand and back to his face. When I finally decide to give him the greeting he was waiting for, he raises his eyebrows. As I watch the corners of his mouth rise along with them, I introduce myself.

"Carolina."

"Hmm... Carolina." he repeats as if to be testing out how the combination of letters in my name roll off the tip of his tongue.

"I like it." He lets go of my hand and in place of it went his guitar. I return to unpacking while he strums on the strings trying to create a new melody.

Individual research.

"We've been walking for hours."

"Where are we going next?"

"When's lunch?"

"Guys. Guys. Check the schedules I gave you. We're covering as much ground as we can, then we're breaking for lunch." Professor Gates says trying to calm everyone down. Who knew college kids could be so immature. They're really getting on my nerves, screaming and yelling at each other, complaining about how they're bored, tired and/or hungry. They're like a bunch of kindergartners. I can't even focus on what Gates is trying to tell us, and I'm in the very front.

As Professor Gates stops the group yet another time to tell a few students to behave, I take time out to search for the library closest to us. Only a block or so away there's one right beside a cafe. When we break for lunch that's where I'm going. I see everyone in front of me starting to walk again. Suddenly, I'm towards the back of the herd just being dragged along.

I think it's a bad idea to start the tours before we even pick our topic. No one's gonna want to listen to any information about anything besides their topic.

Then why are we?

As I make my way to the front again, pushing past people and saying excuse me about a thousand times, I try to get his attention.

"Professor Gates?" I start trailing behind him, but when he doesn't answer or turn around, I move up.

"Mr. Gates?" I repeat, this time louder and from beside him. But again, he doesn't say anything or even stop to answer. He just keeps walking and looking down at his map as if he were in it. I decide to continue regardless.

"I don't think we should do this tour today-" He interrupts me with a deep chuckle.

"You and the rest of the class. Now, go and join the group."

As he starts picking up his pace, I get stuck between a couple other students. He thinks I don't want to do the tour because I don't want to do anything, like the others. But I just want to choose a topic first. It would be much easier, for everyone. Pushing back to the front of the crowd, I try again.

"Professor Gates. I think it would be easier to have us pick our topic and have us do individual research today." He still isn't looking up. I wonder how he even knows where he's going.

"Then we could start tours tomorrow-"

"But you all still would have to make it to every one of these places. With this many students, we're going to need as much time as we can get." He pauses when a crumpled piece of paper flies out from nowhere and goes in front of our faces.

His expression changes from confused to angry as he takes the time out to glare at the boys behind us. He bends down to pick up the paper and says, "If we have to keep stopping on a count of immature actions from your classmates, it's going to take even longer."

Once again, he sends a glare their way and we all continue walking. I have to say something to really get his attention.

"Not if you make a schedule." I suggest. He pauses again this time rubbing the hairs on his chin, thinking.

"What kind of schedule?"

I knew he wouldn't pass that up. For some reason, he really loves creating schedules and agendas, and he loves having people follow them. We start walking again while I tell him what I'm thinking.

"You could let us pick our topic today while you create the schedule..."

"Mhm..." he says while nodding for me to continue.

"...you could assign each day, or a certain amount of that day for a tour. Then have people sign up to go on that tour. The tour for their topic."

He scrunches up his nose and asks me to explain further.

"Okay. Say I chose, Big Ben. I take a look at your schedule and I'd join you, along with any other students deciding to do their projects on Big Ben, to the tour on the day you assigned it."

He furrows his eyebrows and asks, "What about the days that aren't for their topic?"

"Individual research." When I say that, he furrows his eyebrows even more.

"Think about it. It could be a great way for us to learn more, earn your trust and not to mention you wouldn't have to keep dragging around teenagers. You might actually get the chance to enjoy some of this trip."

When the tips of his smile start to increase, that's when I know he had decided to agree. He stops once again, but this time it wasn't to get onto ill-mannered juveniles, it was to give instructions.

"Alright. Change of plans." He pauses to check his watch then says, "It's eleven thirty. We're breaking for lunch early and-"

Before he could finish, a bunch of boys in the back start to get loud and obnoxious.

"And!" he raises his voice. "I expect you all to get back to the dorm by two. Be ready to do some research on your topics."

Everyone was quiet waiting for him to finish, but I think he already has. He gives us a confused and slightly irritated look then says, "Why are you all still standing here? Off with you."

He waves his hands at the crowd telling us to scatter and we do. As I was just about to walk towards the coffee shop I pointed out earlier, that Rian kid comes up to me and pats me on the back.

"Nice one, Tennessee."

Tennessee? My name is Carolina. I'm from Tennessee. So is he.

"It's Carolina..." I try correcting him but he had already walked away with a group of his friends.

Tennessee? Why would I be named Tennessee and live in Tennessee. Who gets named after the state they live in. Then again, why would I be named Carolina. A question only my parents could answer.

When I have children, I'm not- under any circumstance- naming them after a country, state, or city. No, not happening. I think it's odd. Then when you put it together with Taylor, it just sounds weird. Carolina Taylor. I don't think so. That's kind of the main reason I have my close friends call me Taylor. I don't feel comfortable being Carolina.

As I start to walk again, I take out my map. I have the slightest clue on which way I'm going, but I seem to be heading in the right direction. According to the map, if I'm on Oxford Street right now then just around the corner should be the cafe.

Turning right and following the sidewalk around the corner I come across the cafe, and as I pass it to head to the library the smell of freshly baked pastries engulfs me. I have to stop and take in a deep breath. I continue towards the library and when I open my eyes I come face to face with a dark, rickety, old building. This doesn't look like a library.

When I glance back down at the map, I realise it was never a library but an old bookstore instead. It won't hurt to look around anyway. Maybe I'll find an absolutely amazing history book. That would be helpful. Come to think of it, this place looks abandoned. I bet it's closed or shut down.

To my surprise, when I lift the door handle it opens. In fact, it almost swung open on it's own. Normally I wouldn't go near a creepy place like this, but it's on Professor Gates' list.

"These are some of the best places to gather research." he said. So it must be harmless. But when I walk inside, the chilly atmosphere tells me otherwise. I decide to just shake off the feeling and continue.

Walking through the small lobby area where the front desk is, I see no one. Not a soul in sight.

"Hello?" I call out while finding my way to the countertop. On it I see a small bell with a note in front of it covered in a thick layer of dust. I run my fingers over the paper making it visible.

'Ring for service.'

I shrug to myself and tap the bell once. The ringing files throughout the empty space, but no one comes running to my aid. Ring for service, it said. Yeah, right.

So instead of waiting for someone to appear, I decide to look around on my own. There aren't many bookcases. From what I can see, there are only four. But they seem to be brand new, unlike everything else in this place.

I walk through their shelves and decide to check out their selection, which isn't more than a few children's books, some drawing how tos and horror stories.

Why would Professor Gates put this place on the list? It doesn't help. As I look around some more I come across a stairway that leads to what looks like a loft. My curiosity gets the best of me and I carefully head up them. Trying to be quiet, but not really succeeding. These stairs are squeaking with every step I take.

Once I'm at the top I see a much larger selection than what is downstairs. There are more books up here than in the actual store. But there's a big difference between these books and the ones in the shop below.

These books look as though they've never been opened or touched, at least not in a while. They must be old. I wonder if anybody comes up here. I wonder if people are even allowed up here. I'm probably trespassing.

When I start for the bookcases I feel a chill run throughout my entire body, instantly making my stomach drop. This place is strange and it's definitely freaking me out. Let's just get a book and leave.

I slowly make my way over to the first shelf in the line but something stops me. I feel someone's breath on my neck, causing me to hold my own.

Slowly turning around and preparing myself for anything, I see nothing. There's no one there. My heartbeat returns to its normal pace and I start to head back to the books, but I feel like someone's watching me and something's telling me I shouldn't be up here. "I'll just grab a book and leave." I think to myself.

I'm walking through the aisle and I start skimming through every book title, but none of them seem to be what I'm looking for. They would all be helpful, if I knew what my topic would be. I suppose I could just choose one.

As I turn the corner and start looking through the next aisle, I start coughing. These few have a lot more dust than any of the others have and my eyes are starting to water. Maybe I should just leave.

But before I can, a certain book catches my eye.

Dive Into History

Sounds about right. Maybe this is what I've been looking for.

I reach over and pick up the book, wiping off the dust. As I open the front cover I hear a noise making me jump, dropping the book in the process. I quickly turn around and again, find nothing.

When I bend to pick the book up off the floor a deep voice startles me.

"Tourist?" it asks. I snap my head up along with my body. Standing beside me I see a boy around my age, leaning on the bookcase. Curly brown locks and light blue eyes. A much lighter shade than mine. He looks just as shocked or scared as I bet I do.

I regain my breath and answer, "Project."

"Ah." he replies while turning around behind me and grabbing another book. "Try this one."

Without even waiting for my answer, he takes *Dive Into History* from me and places it back in its original spot on the shelf. I watch him as he turns away and bends to blow off the dust. As the little particles fill the air he hands it to me.

"It has more topics to choose from." When he said that, he smiled showing off his deep dimples.

"Oh." I say while reading the cover. "*Guide to England.*"

"Yeah. It has almost every important event that's happened since the early 1700's, and even some urban legends." He reaches over my shoulder and opens the cover. Flipping through it while it's still in my hand, he shows me the index.

"Refer to this as your guide and these are your topic choices." He turns a couple pages until he finds what he's looking for. Still leaning over my shoulder, so close to me that I can smell the peppermint on his breath, he says, "I think this is an interesting topic. If you want my opinion."

I look down and start to read the title of the chapter he pointed out when he beats me to it.

"Duke Robert Price. He's got to be my favorite. It's not all history. It has both historical facts, events proven to be true, *and* urban legends. Some believe them, others, do not. It all depends on the reader, I guess."

I nod and start flipping through the pages, but I can still feel his eyes on me, watching me decide to either take his advice or not.

I close the book and look up at him. That smile was still plastered on his face. Just seeing it makes the horrid atmosphere disappear.

"Thanks." I say while I start walking towards the stairs. I notice him following behind me so I decide to ask how he knew what book to choose and exactly where it was. "Do you work here?"

"Naw, I just come here a lot." I watch him shove his hands into the pockets of his dark blue skinny jeans as we head down the stairs.

When I take the last step, I go towards the counter for check out. Still, no one was there. So I ring the bell again and try to peek my head into the back room, but the door is shut and it's too dark to see through the windows. Since the lights are off, I guess no one's here. I'm just wasting my time.

When I turn around, the boy with blue eyes is still standing there. Still smiling. It was nice he helped me and all, but this is getting kind of creepy. I don't even know his name and he's kind of following me.

Maybe I should just leave. No one's here to check me out anyway. I was right, this place is abandoned. Except for this kid who "comes here a lot".

"Well..." I say while shrugging and placing the book down on the countertop.

"You aren't getting it?" he asks in confusion. Can he not see that no one is here?

"There's no one here." I start but he interrupts me by reaching over and picking it back up.

"Just take it." he says while offering the hardcover to me again. I shake my head and push it away.

"I'm not stealing-"

"It's not stealing if you bring it back. Here. I do it all the time." He tries handing it to me again, but I just look at it.

He lets out a deep breath and hops over the counter.

"Alright." he says leaning down to the computer.

I watch him as he messes with the book and types some stuff on the keyboard. He reaches into his pocket and pulls out a wallet, then a card. After he finishes swiping it, he stamps the book to finish. I thought this place wasn't a library.

"It's checked out under my name on my customer card." I smile at his kind gesture and go to take the book from him when he pulls it back a bit. "I trust you'll bring it back?"

My smile grows a little because of his thick accent and he finally hands me the book. I like this guy. He's sweet. Before I get the chance to debate further about it, I end up inviting him to join me.

"I'm getting some lunch. Do you..." For some reason my words come out slow and confusing, but the smile on his face tells me he understands.

"Sure...yeah." he says trying to climb back over to where I'm at.

"Where do you want to go?" he asks while slipping on his coat and scarf.

"Um, I was just going to check out the cafe next door." I tell him. He nods and beats me to the door so he can hold it open for me.

I give him a smile as I pass and we head next door.

BEING EXTRA CAREFUL.

When the door to the cafe opens and I step inside, the same smell of pastries hits me yet again but this time the strong scent of coffee fills the air as well. What a wonderful smell. That's what my grandmother's house used to smell like before she passed. It reminds me of home. Of Tennessee. As I start to get all emotional, the lady at the counter asks us what we'd like.

"Um. What hot beverage would you recommend?"

"What would I recommend?" she asks shocked like no one has ever cared for her opinion before now. I nod as she looks up at the menu.

"I think I would get the pumpkin spice latte and or the vanilla latte."

"Alright. Then I'll have the pumpkin spice latte and..." I look to the boy that came here with me and he's still deciding. A sly smile comes to his face as he begins to order.

"Then I'll have the vanilla latte." he says while looking down at me.

The lady clears her throat and replies, "Okay. What name is the order under?"

"Carolina." I say as she writes down what she hears. Then she looks up at me, waiting for something. My last name. "Taylor."

After writing it down, she nods and tells us to have a seat and that our order will be ready soon.

"So... Carolina?" he says making sure he gets my name right. I nod as we head to the small table with only two chairs near the window.

Once we get there, he holds out his hand and says, "My name's Robbie."

As I shake it, shivers get sent down my spine. I quickly pull away and he asks, "Is something wrong?"

"No. Not at all." I lie and put on a fake smile. It was a strange feeling. Different. Dark. But I brush the thought under the rug along with any remaining feelings. Then Robbie pulls out my chair for me. As I unbutton my coat and attempt to separate from my scarf, Robbie notices that I was having trouble and offers to help.

But when he touches my shoulders, that feeling comes rushing back. I try my best to ignore it and just focus on what's happening.

Once I'm out, he lays it neatly on the back of my chair and does the same with his.

"Order for Carolina Taylor." A tiny voice calls throughout the cafe. Just as I'm about to get up and go grab our order, he stops me and stands himself.

I watch him walk up to the countertop and take our drinks from the girl.

Shortly after, he returns with two cups. He hands me one and says, "Coffee for the lady."

Even though the thought of his touch scares me for some reason, I can't help but smile.

"Thank you." My whisper was barely audible. I don't know why but trying to talk to him is making my throat close up and my mouth dry. He's odd and I get a strange vibe from him but, call me crazy, I feel somewhat drawn to him.

"So what's the project for?" he asks while lifting his styrofoam cup to his pink lips that have obviously been chapped by the cold.

I take the time to swallow as he watches me intently waiting for my answer. But the more I feel his gaze, the longer it takes for me speak. When I finally get it out, I say, "My college class."

He nods and asks what university I go to. I laughed and say, "I don't."

He gives me a confused look asking what I meant. So I explain further.

"I'm in high school. A senior. I just take a global studies class at a college level."

His dimples re-appear as he starts to smile again.

"Oh. So you're smart?"

I laugh again and say, "Not really..."

"And modest." he says just before taking another drink. I shake my head and in a sarcastic tone he says, "Sure.

"How old are you exactly?" he asks.

"Eighteen." I wonder how old he is. He looks my age, but I don't know. He could just have one of those young faces. Before I can get the chance to ask him his age, he asks me another question.

"And your class just came all the way to England for a project?" I laugh at his comment. As does he.

"Kind of silly, isn't it?"

Now that he's said it out loud, it doesn't make too much sense. It's just a great experience, I guess. It's one of the perks of being in a college class when you're in high school.

"Something on your mind?" he asks pulling me out of my thoughts. I shake my head and my gaze finds its way to my hands.

"Seems like there is."

"It's not important." I start to stand and he does along with me. "Thanks for the book."

He nods and asks, "Will I see you again? Sometime?"

I stop in my place and look up at him. He's just awaiting my answer.

"Hopefully." I say while reaching for my scarf and placing it around my neck.

Before I could grab my coat, he does and holds it up for me to slip into. He sticks his arms around my neck to untuck my hair.

I get that feeling again and almost jump out of my skin.

"Sorry." he says backing away as if he felt it too. I watch him with curiosity as he puts on his own coat.

I think I need to get out of here. Away from him. I thought it was the bookstore that was giving me that feeling, but he was there. Maybe it was him. It was strange how he just appeared. He popped up out of nowhere. Plus, he was the only one there besides me.

I'm just paranoid. There's nothing wrong with him, he's just a sweet guy. But why do I keep getting shivers when he touches me? And they aren't excited shivers either. They're dark and quite unpleasant.

Once he's situated, I head for the counter to pay for our coffee, but he grabs my arm and I'm frozen in place.

"I already paid." He stands there towering over me and stares into my eyes as he waits for my reply. But like I said, frozen.

"When?" I manage to choke out.

"When she called out our order." He finally lets go and a wave of relief washes over me as he walks towards the door.

"Coming?" My eyes shoot over to him and I see that he is holding the door open waiting for me. I nod and head in his direction. Even if I get strange feelings from him, he's a gentleman.

Once I exit the warm shop, a chill runs down my spine. The air became colder as time passed. While I'm walking, I notice Robbie beside me every step of the way.

He catches me staring and asks, "Can I walk you somewhere?"

Part of me wants so desperately to say yes, the part of me that's attracted to the mysterious gentleman with sky blue eyes that I've grown fond of in the past half hour. But the other half of me isn't sure if I should let him know where I'm staying.

I've realised we've stopped walking and he's staring.

"Yes." The word just slipped out. But when it did, his attitude changed. He was holding back a smile; you could easily see the happiness in his eyes. They turned an even darker shade and glazed over in a way that made them shine.

That's gotta be it. His eyes. Mesmerizing, they are. If I am in fact going to see him again, I feel the need to be extra careful around him.

"Do you want to take a cab?" he asks. When I nod, he walks to the edge of the road to flag down a car.

As he does, I drink the rest of my coffee and toss the empty cup in a nearby trash can. Come to think of it, I didn't see him hand the lady any money even though he said he had.

"Ready?" he calls to me holding the car door open for me as well. When I slip in, he smiles.

"Where to?" Robbie and the cab driver look at me waiting for me to tell them where I'm staying.

"UCL campus. Dorm seven, please." Robbie smiles and sits back in his seat. He seemed to be pleased with himself as if hearing where I was staying has been what he was waiting for, which made me feel uneasy.

As I glance out the window at all the other cars, I think back to the cafe. I was watching him the entire time. He didn't hand anyone money. He didn't even take out his wallet, besides in the bookstore. And right after that he shoved it deep down into his pocket, never to be seen again.

Did we just steal two cups of coffee?

Grab a bite?

"I'm starved." Rian says while his stomach growls, as if on cue. I look up from my laptop and see him set down his guitar.

"Wanna get a bite, Tennessee?" He has a habit of calling me that now. I usually correct him but I figured, what's the point. He's going to call me that anyway. It's not like he doesn't know my name either. I guess he just thinks it's funny.

"So..." he says making me come back from my thoughts. "You comin' or what?"

I was about to shake my head and say no thanks when he insists.

"Don't you eat?" Of course I eat. What kind of question is that? I just look at him and he holds out his hand.

"Come on. Let me buy you supper."

...

"Where do you want to go?" I ask while adjusting my jacket.

"Umm..." He looks around as he tries to decide. I watch him as he runs his hand through his short blonde hair, then his eyes start to grow.

"Here." he says as he pulls me into a bar type restaurant. The smell of smoke fills the air. A totally different smell than the cafe I was at earlier.

"Do you want to sit at the bar or a table?" I think about it for a minute then shrug. I honestly don't care.

"It's up to you." I tell him.

Again, he makes that thinking face that is strangely attractive to me. I can't stop looking at him. He's going to start thinking there's something wrong with me. But I can't help but want to know more about this guy.

"Let's get a booth." he says while walking forward. I follow him into the second half of the building and we take a seat at either sides of the table.

"I think..." he says while looking towards the bar. Then he suddenly asks, "What do you want to drink?"

"Um, surprise me." I honestly didn't care what I get to drink either, unless it's alcohol. I expect him to just order two of what he's getting. While he's over at the bar ordering for us, a lady comes up to me and asks, "Can I start you off with a drink?"

Oh, so they do have waitresses.

"We already ordered drinks, but we'll need some menus if you have them."

She nods and puts her pen in her apron as she heads towards the back. She disappears behind a swinging door. Shortly after, Rian comes back with two beers.

"You're eighteen, right?"

"Yes. Thank you..." I give him a reassuring smile even though I don't drink.

"So," he says while swallowing. "I wonder what food they serve here."

He starts to look around again until I say, "The waitress is bringing some menus."

He nods and takes another drink. We sit in silence racking our brains for something to discuss. Is it possible we have nothing in common? You'd think we would, both attending Professor Gates Global Studies class and going on this once in a lifetime trip. But neither of us seem to want to put in the effort of starting a conversation.

The silence is getting awkward. I notice we're both trying very hard not to make eye contact. When he looks at me, I'm forced to look away.

Luckily the waitress comes back with two worn out menus.

"I'll give you two a few minutes." I tell her thank you and she walks away with a giant smile. I hear Rian let out an over exaggerated sigh as he picks up his menu.

"The bacon burger sounds good." he says pointing it out on the menu.

"I don't eat meat." When I look up from my own selection, I notice how big his eyes got.

"You're a vegetarian?" he asks. All I do is nod. That one comment started up a long debate.

...

"No way. You never had a chili cheese dog either?" Rian asks while pushing back his empty plate. I finish swallowing a bite of my salad and say, "Nope."

"Oh my God- Canadian bacon! Please tell me you've tried Canadian bacon!?"

"No. I don't eat meat. No matter what form. An animal is an animal. I don't eat anything with a face."

"That's no way to live..." When he starts going on about the wonders of meat, I can't contain my laughter.

"No, I'm serious. Not eating meat is like... not wearing clothes! It's fine on occasion," He pauses to wiggle his eyebrows up and down, causing me to chuckle. Then he continues, "but it's necessary. You can't go without it."

I lean forward as he continues to talk about how meat is a necessity.

"Why though?" I interrupt. He glances at me like he doesn't understand what I am asking.

"Why does meat have to be a necessity." I say more as a statement. He opens his mouth to speak and further the debate but no words come out.

I feel a sneaky smile form on my face because I know, I got him.

"I know meat and/or meat products are an important part of our diets-"

"Exactly. So how could you-"

"I'm not finished." I tell him. He smiles and sits back letting me continue my thought.

"But there are substitutes for this very reason. You can substitute regular milk with almond milk, soy milk. You can substitute meat, with tofu and other meat like substances. You don't have to murder innocent animals for your own personal gain-"

"But that's what animals were put on the earth for. Food. God put them here so we could kill them when we're in need of food. If we didn't need meat- not a substitute for meat but actual meat- then why would God make it to where our bodies need it to function properly? Why are you trying to defy God?"

"You have the nerve to talk about me defying God when you're going to sit here, in this bar, under God's watch and get drunk? How do you think he feels about that? What is that, your third beer?"

He shakes his head and shoots me a look while lifting the bottle up to his lips. Finishing it he says, "Oh well."

"Yeah. Oh well." I mock him. The air is silent for a second. Until he realises something.

"Hey. You were drinking too."

"Actually," I push the full bottle in front of him and say, "I don't."

I watch him furrow his eyebrows.

"Why didn't you tell me?" he asks with a tight grip on the bottle that was now in front of him. I shrug and tell him I didn't think it mattered.

"Well..." He grabs it and puts the bottle to his lips. I grimaced at how disgusting I imagined it tasted. It had to be warm by now.

"Why are you drinking that?"

"Why not?" he replies.

I shake my head at him and he tells me he'll be right back, he's heading to the restroom.

"Alright." I say with a nod as he disappears around the corner.

While waiting for him to return, I walk up to the bar to order something that I might actually drink. But I don't see a bartender. I can't even find our waitress. The only people here are the drunks passed out on the bar stools beside me. Then I notice a woman walk out of the back with a couple menus.

"Excuse me?" I say getting her attention.

She looks at me and hesitates. Then she finally answers, "Sorry, doll. I'm not working the bar tonight."

Afterwards she hurries off to the other side of the restaurant.

"Thanks anyway..." I mumble to myself. Couldn't she have stopped and helped me? Or at least got someone else to?

"Is there something I can get you?" I hear a deep voice coming from behind me. I slowly turn and see a boy looking down drying a glass. All I am able to see are his brown curls hanging over his eyes, but he looks strangely familiar.

"Yes, can I have a glass-" I pause when he looks up and I see who he is. He's the book guy. I watch a smile form on his face at the recognition, and I feel one on mine too.

"Hey..." I say realising who he is.

"Long time no see, huh?" he chuckles.

"Yeah, so. Do you work here or just hang out here a lot?" He laughs and nods.

"I actually do work here."

"Then do you think you can get me a glass of water?" I ask with a smile.

"I can do that."

I tell him thank you and watch him walk over to the counter behind him to start filling up my glass. He isn't wearing the same thing as earlier. Well, the same blue pair of jeans are hugging his hips but other than that, his overall ensemble has changed. He has on a full black muscle T instead of a white V neck, his red beanie is gone and an apron is tied around his waist.

"Here you are." He places the glass in front of me and smiles. I was about to head to our table when he stops me and asks, "Are you here alone?"

"No. I'm here with my roommate." He nods and lets me head back.

When I get back to the table I see Rian waiting. He looks a bit impatient. When I sit down with the glass of water he asks, "So you drink water?"

I take a drink to answer his question and he slurs, "Wow. Doesn't eat meat. Doesn't drink alcohol. What else do you not do?"

"Hmm..." I say while I think. "I'm not sure what you want me to tell you."

"Forgedd-it..." he mumbles while slurring again. "Let's go home."

I think those drinks finally got to him.

"Lemme get the.. uh the.. money?"

"The bill?"

"Yeah." he mumbles while shaking his head. He gets up and I watch him walk over to the bar. Once he gets Robbie's attention, they talk for a while. It was probably hard for Robbie to understand him. Rian's drunk slurs are awful.

I bet his slurs are getting worse by the minute. All of a sudden, I watch Rian point over towards me and Robbie's gaze follows. A small smile plays on the corner of his lips right before he looks back at Rian.

Robbie nods a couple times, then I see Rian walk back in my direction.

"Your friend's gonna bring the bill." He takes a seat and lays his head down on the table, still mumbling things I don't understand.

Wait, he said, 'your friend'. Did they talk about me?

"Rian? Are you going to be able to walk back to the dorm?" He groans and shakes his head that still lays on the table top. I sigh and stand up to help him get his jacket on.

"Rian, come on." I say trying to get his arm in the sleeve.

"Need some help?" I turn around and see Robbie behind me holding a check booklet.

"Please?"

He chuckles while I move aside so he can help Rian into his coat. I take the opportunity to get my own coat on and take a look at the bill.

I sigh again and reach into my bag. As I bring out my wallet clutch, I mentally tallied how many drinks Rian had tonight. Four, not including mine.

I shake my head and start to take out some money when Rian's hand grabs my wrist.

"You're not payyingg!" he says a little too loudly. I start to tell him it's fine but Robbie stops me as well.

"He's right, Carolina. You shouldn't pay." He glances around and takes the check book. Then he says, "Ya know what, don't worry about it."

Before he gets the chance to walk away I stop him.

"Hey..." He stops without turning around so I step in front of him. I watch him raise his eyebrows asking what I needed, so I reply with a question, "Is that your answer to everything?"

I watch one side of his mouth raise a tad bit higher than the other forming a cute, crooked smile.

"No." he chuckles while running his hand through his hair.

"Well, thanks. But I can pay-"

He interrupts me while shaking his head making his curls go wild. "It's on the house."

"Thank you." I whisper. He smiles and tells me 'you're welcome'.

I give him one last look and walk back over to Rian, who was still passed out on the booth. I roll my eyes.

"Let's go, Rian." He groans as I shake his shoulder. "Rian, come on."

"Where are w-we going?" he stutters as I stand him up.

"Home." He starts mumbling again and I still don't understand a single word. I lay his arm over my shoulder and look over at Robbie. He was behind the bar filling a couple glasses. I hope this won't be the last time seeing him. Well, at least now I know where to find him.

TAKE ME HOME.

Once we get outside, Rian starts walking on his own constantly mumbling as he waddles down the side of the road. To my surprise, I can understand almost everything he is trying to say this time. At one point he starts telling me the history of his past girlfriends, then he changes the topic way too quickly. We somehow even start talking about how he comes home from college and takes care of his little brother because his mom is almost never home.

All of a sudden, Rian loses his footing and nearly takes me down with him.

"Rian!" I groan as his entire weight falls onto my shoulder while he grabs ahold of my head for balance.

I groan again as he pulls himself back up.

"Ssorry Tenn-"

"Carolina! My name is Carolina!" I snap, gaining irritation at not only the fact he keeps calling me Tennessee, but at the fact he felt the need to be so irresponsible while unsupervised. "I live in Tennessee! *You* live in Tennessee! Why do you keep calling me Tennessee? My name is Carolina-"

"Okay, okay. Calm down." he says as he holds his hands up in defense. That's when I realise that we've stopped walking and that he also isn't slurring or stuttering as bad as earlier. I continue to stare up at him as I wait for him to continue.

"Look," he starts. "I didn't think it bothered yyou. You should've just told mme."

I sigh and grab ahold of him, making us link arms so he doesn't fall as we start walking again.

"It's not as big a deal as I'm making it out to be, and it doesn't bother me either."

"Yes it does-"

"No it doesn't, Rian. It's fine; just drop it." I start walking in front of him, leaving him behind until I hear a faint apology.

"What?" I ask while turning to look at him, but he doesn't answer or make eye contact. "What did you say?"

"Sorry! I said I was ssorry, Carolina. Geez." He tries to hurry past me, leaving me behind like I had just done him, but I catch up.

"Ya know," he starts once he notices me beside him. "You aren't likke the other girls I like- er um... I mean in class."

Did he just say...?

"How am I different?" I decide to ignore his slip up and he just shrugs as he continues to mumble stuff under his breath.

"I'm feelin' sick!" He runs into the alley beside the bar and throws up in a trash can. I let out another sigh as I follow after him to make sure he's alright. I was about to rub comforting circles on his back when he turns around and pins me to the wall of the building.

"Rian? What are you-"

"Shh..." He grabs ahold of my waist with one of his hands as the other is tight on my jaw. "I thought since you're a vvegetarian, figure I'd hhelp you outt."

I feel him run his hand down the side of my neck; it lands on my waist along with the other, unbuttoning my coat in the process. He moves the black fabric to the side and lifts my shirt up just a tad to expose a little skin as he squeezes my waist hard enough to leave fingernail marks embedded deeply into my side.

"So vvegetarian," he says while keeping me pinned to the bricks with his chest as he attempts to unbutton his belt. "Ready to taste some meat?"

I honestly cannot move a muscle; I was so shocked by all that was happening. Even if my arms weren't pinned down, I probably wouldn't be able to move. All I'm able to do is watch as the drunk, horny college boy takes advantage of me. And at that thought, tears come to my eyes but they don't fall. I won't let them. I will not show weakness.

He goes to grab my chin, but I nudge him away from my face. I watch as he raises his eyebrows bringing a smile along with it, because this was supposedly funny to him.

I open my mouth to shout for help when he clamps his hand over it, silencing me.

"Don't you dare sscream!" he whispers through clenched teeth.

"It'll be sso much wworse for you if you ddo." he slurs while trying to tug down my jeans. I try pushing my body weight into his chest to get him off me, but he just comes back with more force instantly keeping me immobile. I close my eyes. I can't bear to watch.

"I suggest you let her go."

I hear a deep, raspy voice and my eyes pop open. I turn my head slightly to the left to see Robbie standing at the entrance of the alley holding my scarf and bag in his clenched fist.

"Get l-lost, prick!" Rian yells back trying to return and finish what he had almost started.

"I'm not going to ask a second time." Robbie is now only a few feet away from us. I can see his jaw tighten along with his hands around my personal belongings.

Rian starts to laugh loudly causing me to jump a tad.

"Hey, I g-get it." he says letting go of my waist only to grab the side of my rear. I try to pull away, feeling extremely violated, but that only causes him to tighten his grip and pull me closer to his chest.

"We c-can share." he says staring into my eyes. These few words terrified me.

I don't think Robbie would hurt me like that, but all of those bookstore and cafe feelings started coming back. What happens if he leaves? What happens if he pretends he never saw a thing? What happens if he agrees and joins in?

What happens to me?

SOMEWHERE SAFE.

Rian laughs again while trying a second time to undo my zipper. This time he succeeds and my pants fall loose around my ankles. No matter how hard I try, no matter how much I struggle, he still continues to overpower me.

All of a sudden, something hits Rian over the side of the head making him fall to the ground. I almost lose my balance and join him on the concrete, but something catches me. Robbie.

He is standing beside me with one hand on my arm keeping me in place and the other is still grasping the round object he had just used on Rian. I watch him toss it to the ground causing it to create a loud smash against the other trash cans.

"Come on. Grab your pants. Let's go." he tells me.

I reach down to grab the article of clothing I'm missing and try to speak, but he interrupts me.

"Hurry before he gains consciousness." Robbie grabs my free hand and drags me out of the alley.

After running a ways through the deserted streets to make sure we were far enough away, he finally lets me stop and quickly slip on my pants. I fumble around with the buttons, my hands shaking wildly while trying to catch my breath. Before I could get them completely closed, Robbie takes ahold of my shoulders and holds me back at arm's length.

"Are you alright, love?" he asks. This time when he touched me, I didn't feel afraid or even the least bit strange. I feel safe and comforted.

I nod to answer his question and while wrapping his arms around my waist he says, "Good. Let's get you home."

"Robbie." I say getting his attention. "Rian was my roommate."

I can't go back there. I mean, I guess I could tell the Professor about what happened, but he would lose all trust in everyone, including me, for going out past curfew and drinking. I can't just explain without informing him of our whereabouts.

I then realise that we had stopped walking and Robbie was glancing around the city, looking up at the buildings around us.

"Alright. Here's what we're going to do." He grabs my hand and starts to lead me over to another alley.

"Robbie-"

"Do you trust me?" he asks while squeezing my hand, which is nothing compared to his big ones. I open my mouth thinking an answer would come out, but I stay silent. I look up from our intertwined fingers to his eyes. There's something about them in this moment, something telling me to agree, and that I can trust him.

And with that final thought, I decide to nod my head yes. Without breaking our stare, he smiles and says, "Okay. Then let's go."

He gives my hand a reassuring squeeze and we start to walk towards the alley again.

"Hey Robbie?" He hums to my question so I continue, "Where is it we're going?"

He sighs and runs his free hand through his curls, "I'm going to take you somewhere safe."

"And where might that be?" I ask trying to get a straight answer instead of him beating around the bush.

"You're staying with me at my flat for the night. If you don't mind." I look up at him for what seems like the millionth time tonight and see the most sincere smile I've ever saw.

"Okay." I tell him causing his smile to grow. This is going to be an interesting night. "Hey, did you seriously hit Rian in the face with a metal trash can lid?"

He chuckles and says, "Don't talk about it, okay?"
I snicker to myself as we cross the street to his London apartment.

Woe is me!

"This is the dining table, for your dining pleasures. And the bathroom is through that hall there." I laugh as he points out all the places in his apartment.

"There's the living room area with my brilliant new telly. On Sundays, I watch *The Walking Dead* and if you touch the remote, *you'll* be dead." I continue to laugh as he says, "Just kidding.

"Since you're the guest, you'll take the bedroom and I'll sleep on the couch." I smile at his polite gesture but he really doesn't have to switch for me. I'd be happy crashing on the sofa.

"Um... oh! Now the best part." He grabs my hand and pulls me through the dining area and into the kitchen.

"And this, is where the magic happens." He glances around the room as if he were admiring every old cupboard and worn out tile in this place.

"Ya know, it's not much but it's home." he says with a smile while placing his hand on the counter. A few seconds of silence goes by and you could tell how proud he is of this place. No matter how bad it looked to others, it's a palace to him.

"So. You like to cook, huh?" I ask, breaking him out of a daze.

"Oh. Yeah. I spend most of my time here. Other than reading or working, this is what I do."

He takes a deep breath and lets it out while saying, "But feel free to cook whatever you'd like. What's mine is yours."

He smiles and walks past me towards the bedroom he pointed out not too long ago.

"And that goes for the entire house." He gives me a warm smile and tells me to follow him.

...

He's nice. Sure, he's a tad bit strange, but he's so sweet. I sit awake thinking of the boy in the next room. Why is it that he's been so nice and inviting?

I can't quite put my finger on it, but he gives me a feeling. I really like him. Or at least I think I do. There's one thing I know for sure: he smells amazing. I didn't have any clothes so he offered me one of his t-shirts while he threw my stuff in the wash. The smell of either his cologne or dryer sheets lingers everywhere. On the shirt, on these sheets. All of it smells like the boy who saved me.

I am truly grateful he was there and for what he had done. I don't believe I even said thank you for any of this. For taking me in, letting me borrow his things, invading his privacy like this, and for the most important gift: saving me from Rian.

I wonder if it would be inappropriate to go tell him now.

Before I could even stop myself, and without a further thought, I was up and in the hallway heading to the living room.

When I got there he had on a dim lamp. Guess what he was doing? Reading. I chuckle to myself hoping I don't disturb him, but he doesn't even notice my presence.

I come up behind him and look down at the book he is holding. I can't quite tell what it is. He has it open all the way, reading and following along with his finger.

I lean down on the back of the couch to get a closer look and he jumps a tad.

He slams the book close while swiftly turning around to look up at me. Once he sees it's just me, he calms down.

"Oh, sorry. I thought... never mind." He takes a deep breath and turns back around. "What are you doing up, love?"

"I just wanted to come say thank you for everything from earlier." I say while taking the seat beside him.

He smiles and says, "It's not really a big deal-"

"Yes it is." I firmly interrupt him.

He looks down to his lap so I decide to change the subject. I reach over and grab ahold of the book he was reading while it's still in his hands.

"*A Lover's Complaint*." he says as I read the cover. "It's written by..."

"...Shakespeare." We say at the same time, which brings a smile to his face. A small smile finds its way to mine as well as I let go of the hardcopy and sit back against the couch cushions.

"So you like poetry?" I ask trying to look through the book over his shoulder.

"Yeah. Quite a bit actually. Here, listen to this." He flips through the pages looking for what he wants to read to me. He clears his throat and sits up straight before he reads, which makes me smile.

"But woe is me! Too early I attended a youthful suit- it was to gain my grace- o. One by nature's outwards so commended that maidens eyes stuck over all his face. Love lacked a dwelling and made him her place; and when in his fair parts she did abide, she was new lodged and newly deified."

He puts on his adorable thinking face and turns to face me.

"What do you assume he had meant by that?" I take a deep breath and hold it in.

"What do *you* assume he meant by that?" I say making him glance down and chuckle to himself.

"I'm not certain. He's hard to follow sometimes. That's why I like to decipher each stanza. To understand each line. You've gotta be more thorough with stuff like this, ya know?" he said with such intensity he began to blush.

"Yeah." I smile at him and take another deep breath, this time letting it out. I'm a bit of a Shakespeare nut myself, so maybe I can help him out.

"Here," I say leaning over to look with him. "I don't think it's supposed to be deciphered. It's poetry. Everybody gets something different out of it."

He nods his head yes but waits for me to continue telling him what I think.

"However, if you would like my opinion," I pause to read over the stanza a second time. If he wants thorough, I'll give him thorough.

"*...'early I attended a youthful suit- it was to gain my grace...'* I believe it's saying she listened to the young man whose intentions were to seduce her." I see him nod from the corner of my eyes, so I continue.

" *'o, one by nature's outwards so commended, that maidens eyes stuck over all his face...'* Um, I'm gonna say 'natures outwards' is referring to his external appearance. Basically saying he was so attractive she couldn't take her eyes off him."

I send him a smile and he gladly returns it.

" *'love lacked a dwelling and made him her place...'* Hmm..." I pause to think about it. "This one's hard."

"Can't decipher them all, right?" he playfully smirks. Is he mocking me?

"Maybe," I reply. "Well, what do you think this line means?"

"I'm going to say that, she couldn't find love until she met him-"

I interrupt him on accident with an unsure hum. His eyes meet mine, no matter how hard I was trying to keep from looking at him. His shocked expression scared me a little.

"I didn't mean it like that-"

"Okay. Since you're the Shakespeare genius, why don't you tell me what you think about that line. Go ahead, enlighten me." He smiles and hands me the book.

I slowly take it and watch him lean back to get comfortable. By the smile still lingering on his face, I can tell he's only joking around.

I re-read the line over and over again. I think I've got a pretty good idea of what I think it means, but I'm not sure how to word it.

"Not sure, are you?" I hear Robbie ask.

"Hang on a sec." I try waving him off, but he just leans forwards on his knees and watches me think.

"Okay." I say as a smile forms on my face.

"Okay what?" he asks.

"I've got something." I pivot in his direction.

"Well, let me hear it." I point out each word as I explain my theory.

"I think you were partly correct." He shoots me a proud grin. "But I think he's referring to love not as an emotion, but as an actual human, ya know? Or the idea of love itself. Her love, to be exact."

He gives me a confused look and says, "I don't follow."

I let out a breath and try to explain a second time.

"Okay. Lacked, as in absence or missing. Dwelling, as in residence or place to be stored. So, her love didn't have a place to stay, so it found a place. Him."

"Then she did love him." he states, but I don't feel like that's correct.

"I think she believed she had." I say.

"Okay. Then what thoughts do you have on, *'and when in his fair parts she did abide, she was new lodged and newly defied?'* "

"I think it all depends on how you interpret the last line. For me, based on what I think the 'love lacked' line said, this would mean when her love had settled it was only temporary. Although, renewed? Somehow."

"How do you figure?" he asks.

"Well, I've already read this for one of my poetry assignments-"

"Oh," he laughs. "So you're a cheater."

"No. I'm just saying, the rest of the poem goes on to talk about him deceiving her, along with many other "maidens." Seducing them and convincing them to surrender their virginity." He looks at me with a confused smile, so I start flipping through the book.

"What are you searching for?" he asks, but I just ignore his question and start to read.

"Listen closely," I tell him. " *'so many have, that never touched his hand, sweetly supposed them mistress of his heart. my woeful self, that did in freedom stand, and was my own free simple, not in part, and youth in art, threw my affections in his charmed power. reserved the stalk and gave him all my flower.'* "

I look up from the pages and he's staring at me with a blank face.

"And what's your point, exactly?"

I smile and say, "My point is that that stanza tells you almost everything you need to know. It says he gets into all of the maidens minds. If they haven't actually physically touched him, they imagine it. He's irresistible. He'll seduce you until you crack. He'll make you feel like you're worthless and that he's the only love you'll ever have. He's so charming that it's enchanting.

He uses it on you until your flower is gave. In other words, you surrender your virginity. Then it's onto the next maiden."

He hasn't answered yet, so I think I'm going to finish my thought then go to bed.

"The point of view from the certain mistress or maiden the poem is written by is saying that even though she was free and self-possessive, he somehow still managed to get to her. Now, she's just like all the others."

A moment of silence goes by with him just staring at me, smiling.

"Hey, thanks again for helping me out with Rian earlier." I place my hand on his knee and set the book down on the coffee table. "I should go to bed."

I get up off the couch and start for Robbie's room, his eyes following my every move.

"Goodnight." I whisper over my shoulder and disappear into the hall.

Do I know you?

"More tea?"

"Yes. Thank you." I lift my cup to Robbie and he fills it. I would love to stay here and hang out with him, but I have to get back sometime. I'm just not sure what to do about Rian.

"Thank you for the tea and letting me stay, but I should probably go." I say while standing from the dining room table gathering my things.

I feel Robbie grab my wrist and turn me to face him.

"You can't go back. Not with Rian there waiting for you."

"How do you know he'll be waiting?" I ask. "Isn't there a possibility he won't remember what he had tried?"

He nods and says, "Yes. It's a possibility but-"

"Okay." I interrupt. "Then if there's a possibility it'll be alright, I'm going back. I can't stay here."

"Why not though? At least let me come with you. For moral support."

"I don't know, Rob-"

"Just in case. What if he does remember and tries something? Now that's just as much a possibility as him not remembering." He's not taking no for an answer.

"What about your job? Don't you have to go to that?" I ask, but as soon as I did I realise that was probably a stupid question. I remember him telling me yesterday that the bar only opens at night. It's nearly seven in the morning.

"I'm off today."

Oh, and he's off today. I take a deep breath and grab the rest of my stuff along with his jacket off one of the chairs.

"Come on." I tell him while handing him his coat, which he gladly accepts and slips on.

"But no funny business." I say.

"No funny business?"

We walk out of his apartment and as he locks the door, I say, "Yeah. Don't go in there and try to start something with Rian."

He looks up from the lock and places his hand on his chest.

"I would never." he gasps.

I laugh while grabbing his hand to lead him down the stairs. I really hope Rian doesn't remember. But then again, I hope he does so I can spend more time with Robbie.

...

We get to the school right as the class is leaving the building. I don't see Rian anywhere.

"Maybe he didn't come today?" I imply while looking at Robbie. Or maybe he just chose a different topic at last minute. We walk closer to the group and see the instructor coming towards us.

"Miss Taylor. Where have you been?" he asks while crossing his arms. "You're lucky I didn't contact your parents."

"Professor Gates. I kind of had a problem." I say slightly nervous.

"And what might that be?" I'm getting even more frightened on what he's going to do as a form of punishment.

What should I tell him? I can't just say Rian took me to a bar and tried raping me. Robbie notices my loss for words and begins to explain the situation for me.

"Sir, her roommate Rian got a little drunk last night, and he um, basically tried... he got a little too handsy." he states.

Gates gets a strained look on his face and then speaks to Robbie.

"You? Are her, friend?" he asks him.

45

"Yes, sir. She was with me last night. I heard Rian was her roommate and I didn't feel comfortable with her going back to him for the night." Robbie tells Gates, and I'm so relieved he turned out to be a nice guy.

"Mr. Stevens hasn't bothered to show up this morning. Nor has he checked in with me at all. I wonder if he even returned last night. Perhaps it's best you stay somewhere else?" I nod while he looks around the rest of the students.

"I believe all the rooms are occupied, and there are no vacancies in the dorm. We booked the only ones they had." he informs me.

What if I stayed with Robbie for a few days? I'm not sure if Gates will go for it, but I might as well suggest it.

Before I could, Robbie gets the same idea and says, "She may stay with me. With your permission of course."

I watch Gates shake his head while saying, "I'm not sure that's best."

So I interrupt. There's no way I'm staying here with Rian.

"Mr. Gates. I promise you, I'll get to class on time and my project will be spectacular. I just don't want to be anywhere near Rian." I'm practically begging him, but he still looks as though he's going to say no.

He takes a few seconds to think some more about it and ends up letting out a breath. Then he gives us his answer.

"Alright," He looks back at the other classmates who looked bored out of their minds waiting. "They are not to know, understand?"

I nod but he continues anyway.

"If any of them find out I'm letting you go off campus, they'll all want to leave."

I start to say thank you, but he cuts me off again.

"I'm going to need Mr?"

"Cunningham." Robbie answers.

"Mr. Cunningham. I'm going to need all your information before Miss Taylor is allowed to leave with you."

I smile and Robbie says, "Very reasonable, sir. Thank you, sir."

"Carolina. Take Mr. Cunningham up and gather your personal items." Gates points up the stairs, but before he walks away he says, "Remember. Saturday we're taking a trip to Kensington Palace. That's your topic and I expect to see you bright and early at eight a.m. sharp."

I nod and tell him thank you. When I start to walk away, I hear Robbie saying, "I'll have her here at eight, sir."

"Come on." I say grabbing his wrist and yanking him upstairs.

"Goodbye, sir." he says loud enough for him to hear.

Once we're up a flight or two of stairs, out of the view of the other students, I turn to Robbie.

"Geez. Say 'sir' enough, did ya?" He starts to laugh.

"I was trying to make a good impression."

"Well, I think it worked." We come up to my dorm, so I get out my key. "I don't have much stuff with me so I shouldn't take up too much space, hopefully."

"No, I'm sure you'll be fine." I pause and look up at him. He smiles. That smile is so warm and caring. I think these few weeks will be perfectly fine. I might even get to know Robbie more.

I open the door while saying, "Thanks, Robbie. Really. For everything. Especially letting me crash at your place."

He starts to laugh, but all the noise stops when we see who is sitting on the bed inside. I stop in my tracks, my jaw drops, stomach turning.

"Hey! Where'd you run off to last night?" He sets down his guitar and stands up.

"I had to walk, I think, nine blocks to an empty dorm. Did you get lucky or something?" He's smiling and looking at me.

He starts walking closer, so I back up into Robbie who wraps his arms around my waist causing Rian to finally take notice to him.

"Hey? Do I know you?"

WHO ARE YOU TRUSTING?

"Hurry up and grab your belongings." Robbie whispers into my ear while giving me the push that I needed. Even if it doesn't seem like he remembers what he tried last night, I'm still terrified to be near him now.

I wander over to the closet we had been sharing and grab my smaller bag. "There's no way this will hold everything," I think as I start to search for my luggage. I can feel both pairs of eyes watching me the entire time I struggle.

I look up from the bottom of the closet at them. Rian has a confused look on his face. He takes a step closer, so I take one back into the closet.

"Why are you getting your clothes together?" he asks.

I stay silent. All of those feelings from last night come back when I look him in the eyes. Although he seems like a completely different person right now than last night. He seems lost right now. Last night, he was overpowering me and it seemed he didn't even care. Maybe he liked the thought of being in power. Or maybe he was so drunk he didn't have any control over his own actions.

No matter how much control he had over me, he didn't have control over himself.

"Carolina?" He continues to move closer and closer. Slowly the look in his eyes starts to change. I watch as it goes from the innocent confusion he once had to a devious, suspicious stare.

I can't help but change my mind about him a third time. By the sudden change in his demeanor, I now get the feeling that he knew exactly what he was doing last night, and he remembers it today.

I watch as he picks up his pace. Then Robbie cuts him off by standing in front of me, guarding me from the monster.

"She's just gathering her things to come stay with me for a while." Rian glares at Robbie then looks to me.

"Who's this *prick*?" He points to the only person who seems to care for my safety. By the name he just referred to Robbie as, it was official. He knows exactly what happened last night and he definitely remembers Robbie.

I feel my insides boil with anger of everything this idiot does.

"Robbie." he introduces himself then turns to me. He grabs my wrist and says, "We'll come back for your things later."

We start for the door, but I feel Rian's grasp on my other wrist holding me inside the room. Robbie stops in his tracks and glares in Rian's direction.

"Let go, mate." he tells Rian, but his grip just gets tighter.

"Not until she tells me what's scaring her off." he says staring at me, waiting.

"You!" I blurt out causing him to let go. His facial expression changes and he looks devastated. "Everything you did last night. Everything you tried."

"What are you talking about-"

"Please don't play dumb, Rian. You know you remember." He stares at me with a blank look on his face, like he's trying to recall exactly what had happened.

"No, Carolina. I'm sorry. I don't remember." he tries apologising. Maybe he doesn't remember.

"You really don't-"

"No." he shakes his head.

I look back at Robbie and he was staring at me too. He squeezes my hand that was still enveloped in his and furrows his eyebrows. It seems like he's trying to tell me not to believe Rian.

I turn my head towards Rian again and he looks confused.

"Carolina." He steps closer so Robbie wraps his arms around my stomach pulling me back into him once again. Rian notices how Robbie is holding me and decides to make a comment about it.

"Is he like, your new protective boyfriend? Or something?" He looks down and starts twiddling his thumbs.

That's when I remember what he almost revealed last night, making me feel bad.

"No. He's just a friend." I remove Robbie's arms and march towards Rian who's now watching me. "You really don't remember?"

He shakes his head slightly and tells me the last thing he remembers is learning that I was a vegetarian. If that's true, then he probably doesn't remember meeting Robbie either times.

I let out a deep breath and say, "I'm sorry. We never should have went to that bar."

He looks confused but apologises anyway.

"No. I'm sorry. It was my idea. Besides, I should've controlled my drinking."

I think I'm going to believe him, but that doesn't change the fact that Rian tried raping me last night.

"If I may ask," Rian interrupts my thoughts. "What did I do?"

I hear Robbie let out a disgusted noise. When we both turn to look at him, his gaze immediately hits the floor as he shoves his hands into his pockets.

"We can talk about it later. But right now, I have to gather my stuff." I say while putting some clothes into my bag.

"Why can't we talk about it now?" he asks. I shrug and finish getting the rest of my clothes.

I walk over to my desk and pack all of my school equipment into the smaller bag I found earlier. When I look up, both eyes are watching me again.

"Goodbye, Rian." I walk past him and Robbie closes the door behind me.

"Thank you." I tell Robbie as he takes my luggage from me and carries it himself. When we get to the lobby, the group of students, along with Professor Gates is long gone.

"Hows about we drop your stuff off at mine, then grab something to fill you. Yeah?" I nod with a smile as I get into a cab.

Looking back, I see the college campus getting smaller and smaller. Suddenly, I feel like I've made a huge mistake.

I don't know this guy and when I met him, he was hanging out in an old abandoned bookstore. I glance towards him and he's staring out the window, smiling.

Did I just choose to trust the wrong person?

EXPERIENCE?

I continue to stare at Robbie as he drives to get food. His features are hypnotizing, but I can't help but think he's dangerous so I don't want to somehow get attached. I can feel his gaze on me as I continue to daze. Suddenly, he smirks.

"I asked you a question, love." he says, content at the fact I was staring at him.

"Oh, sorry. What was the question?" I ask sort of embarrassed.

"I asked what you were like. I figured, since you're staying with me for a while, we should get to know each other more." He looks nervous while waiting for my reply.

"What do you want to know?" I ask.

He shrugs and says, "Tell me about yourself."

"Anything?"

"Everything." he replies.

I take a deep breath and stop to think. I guess I'll start with the basics.

"Well. I live in Tennessee with my father and my mother. But I desperately wish I had a little sister. To boss around, ya know?" I hear him chuckle although I was kind of serious.

As I thought about the next thing to tell him, I start to feel the same chill I got earlier in the bookstore. Without thinking, I tell him I'm afraid of ghosts.

"Ghosts?" He furrows his eyebrows and leans in closer to me.

"Yeah. I hate being scared. I can't even sit through a scary movie without," I pause while thinking back to the last time I watched a scary movie. The only time, really.

I believe it was during the summer sometime a few years ago. It was at my neighbor's party. She invited me along with a bunch of other girls. Annabeth, was her name. She was my childhood best friend. But when we got into high school, we drifted apart. More like ripped, actually. She started hanging out with groups of teens that wore all black and cut class to go smoke and drink on the football field.

She wanted to impress them. So, me being a "goody two shoes Christian", I didn't fit in with her and her friends anymore. So I started focussing on school instead of friends. Or boyfriends. Or anything else really.

Then, all of a sudden I got that invite out of the blue. She told me she was done with that stuff and that she wanted to get back to the way it used to be before. But her younger sister told me differently.

'Don't let her lie to you, Taylor. Mom made her invite you. And she still does spells and all that weird black magic stuff.'

But, I decided to show up anyway. Why not? Maybe I could hang out with her sister if Annabeth started getting weird, or I could always go home. To be honest, I had a huge crush on her older brother. That was until he helped her and all the other girls prank me. I'm fine with the harmless pranks usually, but not the ones that are meant to hurt people.

While we were watching *The Conjuring*, I was already beyond terrified and to make it worse, Annabeth and all her friends had left the room to go take care of various things. 'I'll make more popcorn.' 'I'm running to the bathroom.' 'I'll get more blankets.' Pretty soon, it was just me on the couch, scared out of my mind.

"Guys?" I yelled while hugging my blanket. Just before the demon jumped from its hiding spot in the movie, I heard a couple of the girls screaming. So I ran upstairs to see what had happened.

When I walked into the hallway, everything got silent.

"Annabeth?" I called out, and then the lights went off. I felt someone's breath on my neck so I bolted towards Anna's room, where I found her. She was sitting in the middle of her floor with lit candles surrounding her.

"Annab-"

"Shh." she interrupted. "They're coming."

She began glancing up towards the ceiling, and when my gaze started to follow hers, I saw a cloud of smoke rising from underneath her closet door.

"What is that?" I screamed. All Annabeth did was calmly rise from her seated position and walk up to me.

"Open it." she whispered.

"Um, no thanks. Anna, it was nice of you to invite me but-"

"Open it!" she demanded. Honestly, I was extremely scared, but also curious. I slowly let go of the blanket I was holding onto for dear life and grasped the handle.

It creaked as it opened, but when it did, I saw her brother Damien covered in what I assumed was blood, hanging in the closet.

I screamed and backed away from the closet causing me to fall backwards onto the ground.

"I needed him. A sacrifice." Annabeth started slowly walking towards me. Trying to create as much distance between us as possible, I was scooting back.

"Don't worry, Carolina. They have a special plan for you." Her smile was eerie as scratching noises started to fill the entire room. Coming from all different directions.

I got up off the floor and ran downstairs. Eventually out the front door.

As I was heading home, I heard a couple of girls laughing and screaming things out Anna's bedroom window.

'Run home you little baby!'

'She's such a geek.'

Then they started taunting me by singing, 'Goody two shoes! Goody two shoes!'

"I think what scared me the most is that she called me Carolina." I finish off my story. "She never calls me Carolina. She's always referred to me as Taylor."

"Taylor?" Robbie questions.

"Yeah." Actually, she was the one who started the whole 'Taylor' thing in the first place.

"Do you believe in possession?" I turn towards him as I ask. I watch a small smile form in the corner of his mouth.

"No. Ghosts can't possess others." He let out a chuckle.

"Well you sound quite confident in your answer." He starts to laugh. "Seriously. How are you so sure?"

"Uh, I guess I just have a lot of experience with ghosts."

"Experience?" I ask.

He stares at me for a few seconds with a scared expression on his face. Then he turns away and looks out the window.

"Um, so. Where do you want to eat?" He tries changing the subject.

"Robbie." He turns back towards me. "What do you mean experience?"

"Nothing. Just forget I said anything." The rest of the ride is quiet. We decide to order pizza and stay in the rest of the night.

That was odd. Experience as in he does research on them or he messes around with them, like Anna.

Right now he's in the shower. So I have a few minutes to myself to put my things away and think.

That conversation is definitely not over. I'm too curious to let him brush it under the rug. He's the one who wanted to get to know each other. He brought it on himself.

Besides, if I'm going to live here, I'd like to know what goes on in this apartment. I'd like to know who I'm staying with.

DREAM.

"Carolina." I hear a whisper and I groan while turning over in Robbie's bed.

"Hey. Carolina." It's louder this time so I slowly open my eyes and see Robbie sitting on my bedside.

"It's time to get up." he says staring at me. My alarm must have not gone off.

I sit up and palm my eyes, ridding myself of the remainder of sleep I had.

"What time is it?" I look up at him and notice that he's holding something. The book.

"Why do you...?" I start to take it from him and he moves his hand back. I stop moving forward and give him a confused look. "Robbie?"

"You can't touch me. It won't work." He looks devastated.

"What are you talking about?" I go to touch his shoulder and prove him wrong, but he moves back again.

"You can't. Not here." he whispers.

"What are you talking about?"

"Look. You have to wake up." he tells me while lifting up off the bed.

"Robbie. I am up-"

"Just remember. Duke Robert Price." he interrupts me. He clutches the book so tight that his fingers start to turn white. His entire body looks sort of pale as well.

"Robbie, you're scaring me..."

He sits back down beside me and hands me the book. I slowly take it, but when both our hands were on either end, I get that feeling again. It's an eerie feeling and I don't like it.

I think he felt it too because he quickly lets go of his end. He looks on edge.

Then his gaze shoots up to the ceiling as a giant wind blows throughout the room, sending papers all over the clean floor.

"You have to wake up." he says in a more urgent voice while standing again. He looks frightened, but I'm at a loss for words.

"What are you talking about? What's happening?" I manage to choke out.

He looks around the room as the wind begins to blow again. Then he rushes over to me, reaching out to grab me by the shoulders and shake me, but the strangest, scariest, saddest thing happened.

When his hands reach out for my shoulders, they somehow slip through my entire body like I wasn't even real. Like he wasn't.

"It'll never work." he tells himself. Then he looks up to me and tells me to remember, "Robert Price. twenty six: thirty two: forty one: twelve."

A worried look comes to his face and that's when I start to hear the beeping sound of my alarm clock. He tells me to "go" because I "can't stay here".

I rise in my bed to the sound of my alarm clock coming from the side table. I turn it off and sit up in bed just thinking about the dream. Was it supposed to mean something?

I've had nightmares before, but this time was different. It felt real.

I try to shake it off and go get ready for the day, but when I get out of bed, I see that the room has been trashed. Papers are scattered all over the floor. Just like my dream.

TRYING TO HIDE.

"What's going on?" I ask myself. I get out of bed and make my way into the living room.

"H-hello?" I call out, nervous that Robbie would reply.

"In the kitchen, love." I hear his deep voice echoing throughout the hallway. I'm a little hesitant before walking into the kitchen to find Robbie beside the stove.

"I've got breakfast goin', if you want some before you leave." he says not looking up from the task at hand.

"It's about ready. Just have to finish up the bacon-" His smile drops when he glances up at me.

"What's wrong, love? You look frightened." he flips what was in the pan but never takes his eyes off me.

"Um..." I stutter. "Nothing."

I was about to walk into the dining area when I think that maybe I should ask him about the dream.

"Were you in my room last night? I mean, your room last night?" I ask, looking to the ground, but I lift my head up when I feel Robbie's gaze on me. He looks kind of nervous before smoke starts rising up from the pan.

"No!" He turns off the stove and quickly sets the pan in the sink letting out an irritated sigh as he does so.

"I burnt it." he says while staring down at the burnt crisps in the sink. He starts shaking his head while resting his chin in the palm of his hand. With a very disappointed look on his face while leaning on the counter, he lets out another sigh.

"Robbie?" I get his attention. He looks up at me and shakes his head.

"No. I didn't." he answers my question.

"Are you sure? I could've sworn." Remembering everything that happened in my dream made me start to rethink. The wind, Robbie not being able to touch me. Literally, it's not possible.

I notice that I haven't said anything and he's just staring at me with a worried expression on his face.

"Carolina, I don't know what you're talking about?" he states in the form of a question.

"Sorry." I shake the dream out of my head for now and walk up beside him. "Do you mind if I go get in the shower?"

"Yeah. Go ahead. There should be towels in one of the cabinets." I watch him pour a glass of orange juice, then I start back into the hall.

Before I leave completely, I turn towards him and ask, "Do you still want me to leave?"

I watch him furrow his eyebrows and shake his head.

"What gave you that idea?" he asks.

"I don't know. I just thought... never mind." I shrug and head into my room to pick out my clothes.

'Go! You can't stay here!' His deep, scared, raspy voice echoes throughout my head. If he doesn't want me to leave, and he didn't go into the bedroom last night, then it definitely was a dream.

But that doesn't explain the papers or Robbie's room being trashed when I woke. I walk into the bathroom and set the water to how I like it. It's about six-forty a.m. so I have more than enough time to get ready.

When I take off my shirt, it reveals something unexplainable. I look closer into the mirror, and on my shoulders I see hand prints.

"What?" I whisper to myself. I run my fingers over the red markings and it stings causing me to jump a tad.

I do a little turn and see the entire print. The palm is on the back of my shoulder blade and the thumb print is on the front of it. Red, irritated skin burning to the touch. It's sore and I don't know why I hadn't noticed it earlier in the kitchen.

I know it wasn't there last night. Last night? Last night! The dream. Robbie tried grabbing me. I thought it was just a dream.

Well, obviously not. If he was in the room- even if he said he wasn't- and there are hand prints where he grabbed me- even though he couldn't- then the wind, the noises, the fact that Robbie couldn't touch me was real. But I was sleeping?

So, how did all that happen? He told me something. Robert Price, and some numbers. Twenty six: thirty two: forty one and twenty one? Or twenty two? Maybe twelve? I wish I could remember.

But what are they for? Why did he want me to know them? More importantly, if it wasn't just a dream- and I have proof, it wasn't just a dream- then why did he lie about it? What is he trying to hide?

My only hope.

'And so it goes. This soldier knows. The battle for the heart, isn't easily won.'

The train ride is so quiet, you can hear the faint music playing clear as day in the background. Although, the sky outside isn't clear at all. Not even a little bit. Clouds fill the dark sky outside the train window and thunder rumbles shaking the entire car. Is it safe to be on a train in the middle of a storm?

As I continue to over exaggerate in fearing for my life, I start to hear the pitter patter of raindrops. Tapping my foot to the rhythm, Professor Gates tries getting our attention.

"Class. We're going to push everything back a day or two." I hear a couple people sigh in relief as I glance out the window. All I see is pitch black; it was that dark.

"I think we'll reschedule for Thursday. That is if the rain stops. If not, perhaps we can go to a museum of some sort. We're going to ride back around and continue with our individual research today, sorry."

I mentally roll my eyes at the thought. I don't feel like doing my own research. I know I was the one who suggested it, because it seemed like a good idea at the time to be more organized, but who cares?

I wonder if Robbie's still up or if he went back to sleep. That's probably what I would do.

All of a sudden, the train car jerks forward and I'm flung from my seat. Me along with a couple other people are now lying on the floor of the car.

"Attention passengers!" a voice comes over the speakers. *"We're having some technical difficulties due to the weather."*

He sounds hesitant and scared.

"Please hold tight and be patient as we try to start the engine back up again."

"Are you alright miss?" An older man helps me up off the ground and clears off a seat next to him. I sit down, and while dusting myself off again I say with a smile, "Yes. I'm fine, thank you."

A loud beeping noise fills the car causing us all to cover our ears until the same man comes over the speaker again.

"Sorry for the interruption, again. But at this time, would all passengers find the emergency belts and fasten themselves into place. Those passengers standing please be sure to hold onto the emergency bars. This could get bumpy."

I reach over my shoulder and fasten the belt into place. I can hear Professor Gates giving his students the exact same instructions and helping them locate their safety belts. The rain volume grows even more intense, bringing the lightning along with it. I don't have a very good feeling about this.

I reach down and grasp the edge of the chair I'm on. I'm holding on for dear life as the train starts to shake once again. I can't help but think about Robbie. He's honestly the closest person to me here in England right now, not considering the strange dream and behavior earlier.

The train shakes again, harder this time, and everyone jerks forward. You can her a couple girly squeals coming from around the car. That beeping sound comes back and some red emergency lights start blinking.

I squeeze my eyes shut and try to focus on something else. Trying to be somewhere else, possibly my happy place. I hold my breath, but all I can focus on are the conversations of the people beside me. There are people on their phones talking about what's happening, there's a little boy telling his mother that he's scared, and a couple girls in the corner praying.

I close my eyes again when the shaking gets even more rough. My heart starts beating louder than before. It feels like we're going to crash.

"Hold on..." I hear a calm voice whisper to me but when I open my eyes, everyone is scared and worried. We hit another bump as the thunder outside grows. I suck in a sharp breath and tighten my grip.

"It'll be okay. Just hold on." I hear it again, but no one around me said it. I close my eyes and see an image. It's the silhouette of a boy with a head full of curls, but I can't see his face.

"Just a little longer." he says trying to reach down for my hand, but he misses. He can't grab it. He can't grab me. Just like in my dream. With that realisation, I immediately know who it is.

"I won't let anything happen to you." I can hear the smile in his sweet voice, calming me instantly. Then the image of him disappeared. Robbie was here. I don't know how, but he was, and he made me feel safe. He gave me comfort.

That feeling disappears as soon as I hear a couple deafening screams from the back of the car. I open my eyes and my head shoots in the direction of the sound. My heart starts pumping when I notice the sparks coming from outside the window. I knew the storm was bad, but not this bad. I didn't know it was bad enough to make the train car malfunction.

It definitely answers my previous question; it's not safe to be on a train in the middle of a storm. Not safe at all.

The car continues to shake and the fear inside me continues to grow. I get jerked to the side and bump into the older man that helped me earlier.

"I-I'm sor-ry." I shutter out of fear. He gives me a look of pity and starts to stutter himself.

"It's-s alr-right mis-s." He seems just as afraid as I'm positive I am. I glance down at his hands that are wrapped up tightly in an old handkerchief. His skin looks as though almost all of the blood has been drained out.

I reach down and lay my hand over his, to calm his nerves. He smiles lightly, although I can still see how rattled he is.

"It's a-alright-t. We'll-l get thr-rough thi-is." I tell him as sweetly as possible.

The look in his eyes begins to change and he turns his hand to grab mine. He squeezes tight and starts to speak. When he did his stuttering was gone, and before he sounded French.

"I know you will." he whispers in an English accent.

"You m-mean we-e both w-will."

He begins to shake his head, "No, love. I might not."

I start to get confused and even more frightened. When I try to pull my hand away, he holds on tighter.

"Listen to me." he says. "You will be okay. You will. I'm not going to let anything happen to you."

At first I was nervous about the train and I didn't process exactly what he said. Then it clicked.

"W-what?" I feel him run his thumb over the back side of my hand and to be completely honest, I'm getting a tad creeped out.

"You're my only hope, Carolina."

"How-w do y-you-"

"Hold on tight." he interrupts me while squeezing my hand and tucking a loose strand of hair behind my ear. The beeping stops and so does the train causing everyone to fling backwards.

The people who were standing are now on the ground. The fortunate ones on the seats only get a small shove. My body jerks forward then back again, and when it does, my head crashes against the window knocking me out almost instantly.

...

All I can see is darkness. All I hear is another beep, but not the same beep like the emergency beep from the train. This one is less hectic; it's a lot more calm. It goes at a slow rhythm with two second intervals. Then it grows, getting louder and louder in one continuous beep. Suddenly, a light comes into view.

I'm forced to squint my eyes because it's so bright, but I'm drawn to it. It seems to make me happy, like it's calling to me. I take step towards it and it only gets brighter. Then my eyes start to adjust.

"No! Carolina!" I hear a voice calling from behind me, but I can't stop moving closer, and I don't dare look away.

"Stop! Don't look at it!" it says again.

Suddenly, I don't care. I know it's still calling for me but eventually, I can't hear it.

The closer I get to the light, the softer the voice gets. Pretty soon, it fades away completely and I can feel my worries start to fade away as well. It's like an enormous weight is lifted off my shoulders.

I feel like I've just laid down in my bed after a long day at college, like satisfying my hunger, or the feeling you get from helping someone who was in desperate need of a hand. I feel rested, satisfied, accomplished. I feel safe.

Until my curiosity of who the voice belongs to gets the best of me and causes me stop. The safety starts to disappear, getting smaller as I'm being dragged away.

Everything starts rushing back: the weight, the worries, the guilt, then the voice.

"You have to stay with me." By now the light has gotten so small, I can barely see it. I definitely could no longer feel it.

"You're my only hope, please!"

'My only hope', it said. 'My only hope.'

"Robbie?" I turn away from the speck of light and see him just standing there in the darkness. He looks scared at first, but then he smiles.

"I told you I wasn't going to let anything happen to you.

"Follow me..." He waves for me to continue towards him. I start to turn around and make my decision but he stops me.

"Don't turn around!" he says. "You can't look back."

"Why? What's going on?" I ask. He just says the same thing he had previously, but this time he was calm about it.

"Not now." As he's staring into my eyes, I catch the glimpse of a secret. One he wants so desperately to tell me but can't. Something won't let him; *someone* won't let him.

I feel a burn on my wrist so I glance down. I see a deep cut with gushing red liquid. It goes across my wrist and trails up my forearm.

"Here. Let me see." I try handing him my arms, but his hands go through mine. He frowns and leans his face towards my wound. He begins to hover above it because he can't touch me completely. The reason why, I'm still unaware of.

I watch him leave a sweet kiss on the air above my sore spot, and it feels as though he had kissed me entirely.

"I can't think of what else to do." he whispers and brings his head back up revealing to me his big, blue puppy dog eyes.

"Let's get you out of here, love." He bobs his head in the direction behind him. Even though all that's behind him is darkness, I decide to follow him anyhow.

Promise you won't leave?

The beeping is back. Slow and steady.

It seems to be matching the rhythm of my heartbeat and the pace of my breathing. Am I still on the train? As time goes by, I can feel myself slowly coming back together. I can feel that I'm on a bed, and there's something attached to my nose. The aching that was in my arm is now gone, but it appears to have moved up to my head. It doesn't just feel like a headache. It must be from when I hit the window.

I feel my eyes flutter open, and the first thing I see are curls. Beautiful brown ringlets. Then I see eyes, blue ones.

All of the features start coming together and start becoming even more and more familiar. Soon, I start to recognise who's before me. Robbie.

"Hello, love. How are you feeling?" I ignore his question for now and take a moment to look around the room. White walls, big space, medical supplies. I'm in a hospital.

"What's going on?" I ask, though he still hasn't answered me from the first time I asked.

I look back towards him and he's smiling.

"You're at the hospital. But you're going to be okay, like I told you."

"What?" Is he trying to tell me that it was all real? Everything? Every weird thing?

"Where's Professor Gates?" He smiles again and says, "He's next door checking on another student."

My memory is starting to come back and I remember the train. I remember the emergency lights and the beeping, the scared child and the older man. Then Robbie, but I decide to let that go for now. He said he'd tell me when he could, which is later.

So I ask a different question, "Did anyone get extremely hurt?"

He chuckles and says, "No. Not at all."

I give him a confused look and he explains further.

"The only two that are checked into the hospital are you and some other student. He's supposed to stay tomorrow. You can go home in the morning."

"That's good." I let out the breath I'd been holding in causing him to chuckle again. I wonder how long I've been here.

"What time is it?" I ask.

"About..." he pauses to check his watch, then says, "Five-forty."

I'm shocked when I realise how long I've actually been here. We left on the train around nine in the morning. That's almost nine full hours of me being unconscious. And to think, Robbie has been here the entire time.

"Robbie?" I look back to him and he's just staring at me.

"When?" I ask.

I watch him raise his eyebrows as his smile comes back.

"When what, love?"

Something about the way he's acting makes me feel like he knows exactly what I'm talking about, but I feel way too tired to try and explain or play games with him right now.

I shrug and avert my eyes to the white sheets on the bed.

"Later." I hear him whisper. While nodding my head, I feel him grab my arm. He turns it around revealing the cut I had earlier. It looks almost healed. Although, there is a red mark across my wrist, like a handprint.

"I'm sorry, doll." He starts to rub his thumb around my wrist where he had left the mark. "I'm not sure why that happens."

"Me either." I pull my arm away from him, and he furrows his eyebrows. Obviously, he's confused by my reaction.

"I don't feel comfortable around you." I decide to just come out and say it. "I thought I was, but with all these secrets and the strange things that have been happening..."

I shake my head and he stands up. At first I think he's going to leave, but he doesn't. He sits down on the edge of my bed.

"I'm sorry. I'm just trying to keep you as safe as possible-"

"Why though? What's going on?" I say interrupting his apology.

I watch him run his hands through his hair and take a deep breath. Then, he looks around the room.

"Alright." He gets off the bed and closes the door. When he turns back around, the expression on his face scares me. "Promise me you won't leave?"

"I won't, unless you give me a reason to." I whisper, immediately regretting it after.

"Just, promise me?" he snaps back. His expressions are getting even more fierce, but not in an angry way; in a desperate way, like he needs me to say, 'yes, I won't leave you'.

"I need to hear you say it. You won't leave me no matter what I tell you. Promise?" I think about it for a minute. He looks scared and worried, but I can't make any decisions when I don't know what's going on.

After a lot of thinking, I finally say, "I can't make promises to secrets I don't know about. I just won't."

He sighs in annoyance and finally begins to calm down a bit.

"Fine. But you have to listen to it all. No matter what I tell you, or who I talk about. Okay? Can you promise me that, at least?" he says while looking straight into my eyes. I nod my head and he begins to speak.

"It's a long story. Are you sure?" he stops himself.

I take a deep breath and say, "Of course."

I watch the corners of his mouth widen at the slightest as he moves closer to me.

"I guess I should start with where I actually live..." he hesitates. I furrow my eyebrows in confusion.

"What do you mean, where you actually live?"

"I don't live in the complex we're sharing. I mean, I do but I don't. I used to live in Gloucester and I still do.

"Well, I grew up in Sproston Green, but once my mother got remarried, we moved." He pauses to check out my reaction, but I'm just confused. He used to live in Gloucester and he still does? I was doing research earlier and I remember reading that Gloucester is almost three hours from here. So there's no way he lives there.

I watch him run his shaky, nervous hands through his hair again.

"Um... my name's not exactly Robbie Cunningham either." I furrow my eyebrows even more and move back in my bed a little, creating space between us.

"What do you mean, not exactly?" I ask. He takes a deep breath and gets up to sit next to me on the bed again.

"Robbie is short for Robert, and if I wanted to be around people again, I had to change my name without completely changing it-"

"Wait. What do you mean be around people again?" I interrupt him. He looks at me with a worried expression.

"Please, just listen to everything and ask questions later. I'll gladly tell you everything you'd like to know, as long as you listen first."

I nod and sit back on the headboard letting him continue.

"Okay." He takes another breath and starts again. "My mother, Anne, took my father's last name, Cunningham. And that's who I was when I was younger. Robert Cunningham.

"Then she met Walter Price. He was..." he hesitates.

"He was?" I try to encourage him to carry on. I can tell that this is hard for him. All of this hurt him in some way.

"He was Duke at the time, and his brother was in line for the throne." He pauses again to see how I'm taking in all the information, but my expression hasn't yet changed.

"They had secret encounters for weeks until they got caught, and it wasn't likely or proper for The Duke to be hanging around with a poor woman from Sproston Green. So she was punished.

"We were removed from our flat, and traveled quite a bit; due to the fact we no longer had a home. I was only eleven." I can feel my confusion slip away and turn to sadness. Poor Robbie.

"A few years or so later, I remember being in a line waiting to buy fresh bread when we heard the news. Edmund, the new king, had been killed. But Walter was next in line to take his place.

"Not long after we found out, my mother got an invitation to a ball being held at the castle-"

"Castle?" I interrupt. "Robbie, what are you talking about?"

"Questions after. Remember?" I let out a sigh and nod. Then he picks up right where he had left off.

"She attended the party, and the next thing I knew, we were moving into the castle. It turns out his coronation was the following month, but he needed a queen and he chose my mother. Out of all the eligible maidens in Gloucester, he chose her."

I feel like he's lying right to my face. Duke? Castle? He was talking about balls and buying fresh bread. I buy my bread packaged in a store.

"But my mother said we were a packaged deal. Wherever she went, I went. Although Walter wasn't very happy about that, he agreed.

"Are you okay so far? You're alright; you follow?" he asks. I hesitate but reply, "Yeah. I follow."

"Good. Um... my mother became Walters's queen. Therefore I, was royal. Not by blood, but marriage-"

"Wait, you're royal? A prince?" I sit forward and he starts to remind me about when to ask questions.

"Robbie. I don't think I can wait. You said it yourself, it's a long story." I'm starting to get excited. It's cool knowing somebody royal. It's like knowing a celebrity.

"Okay. Tell you what we're going to do. I'll answer a question every five minutes..." He starts setting his watch but I stop him.

"One minute." He looks up from his wrists and there was a cheeky smile plastered on his face.

"Three. And not a minute less." He smiles again and finishes setting his watch to the decided three minutes.

"Alright. Where was I?" he asks, but before I could answer he remembers.

"Oh. Okay. I was about fifteen when I was crowned and everything changed. The castle was huge, clean and I never had to lift a finger.

"I remember Walter calling me into his chambers for a "talk". He said he was no longer Duke of Gloucester, and since I was growing to become a very respectable young man, he wanted to pass the title down to me. Once I turned sixteen, he would. But until then, I trained.

"I just basically got ready to hold the honor of becoming Duke. And eventually, I did. We had gotten exceedingly close throughout the years. Although I wasn't too fond of him as a person- and he is not my father- he was a wonderful king." He was interrupted by the beeping of his wrist watch.

I feel a smile grow on my face; I know exactly what I want to ask.

"Alright. My first question is, Gloucester. What do you mean by 'I used to live in Gloucester and I still do?'" He scrunches up his face as I finish my sentence.

"I was afraid you'd ask that." he says while running his hand over the nape of his neck.

"I used to live in Gloucester with my mother, Walter, his daughter and the help; maids and other aides. I'll get into this later but I ran away to London when I was eighteen. I've been here ever since."

"So technically, you don't still live there."

He smiles at me and says, "I'll answer that... in three minutes."

He clicks his timer and continues.

"I took on the responsibilities of Duke for a while, until a certain incident occurred and I was forced to leave town."

"Okay. I'm sorry, but I can't wait three minutes. You wanted me to listen to everything, so you should tell me everything. What was the incident?" I watch Robbie take a deep breath making his chest rise then fall.

"Well, supposedly someone had tried to murder Walter. And it was believed to be the same individual who had killed the previous king- Edmund- as well.

"But I don't believe that. And neither did my step-sister, Gasmine. She was the only one on my side. My own mother didn't even believe that I..." he pauses. As I wait, I see something go through him. Something that scared me.

This is it. This is what he was supposed to tell me, and he was going to, until he stopped. What made him stop?

"It's okay." I whisper while designing patterns on his shivering hand that I had just grabbed previously. He gives me a friendly smile and begins to tell me what he's been trying to tell me this entire time.

"I'm not what you think I am."

I furrow my eyebrows just as the timer goes off. Both our gazes seem to shoot towards his watch on the wrist I was holding. Now's my chance to ask him.

"Then what are you?" He looks up at me in worry. "And I promise, I won't leave you."

A small wave of relief flashes through his eyes before they return to the worried state it seems he's been in this entire time. He let out a breath, and I feel his grip on my hand grow tighter.

"I believe I'm a ghost."

How'd you die?

"What do you mean you believe you're a ghost?" I let out a laugh thinking it's a joke.

"There are four things that I could become. And I know I'm no longer human." he says just as confused as I am. My smile fades away when I see his face.

"That explains a lot." I start, and he nods.

"I know."

"Wait. You can't be a ghost. How can I touch you?" I ask while holding up our intertwined fingers.

"That's what I'm not sure of. Ghosts can't physically touch humans and they can't possess others."

"But you had." I finish his sentence and he knew exactly what I meant.

"I wouldn't call what I did possessing." he argues.

"Then how would you define what you did to that older fellow on the train?" I ask.

"Hmm..." he thinks. "Persuading?"

"Persuading?" I repeat.

"Yes. I'm able to picture someone in my mind and make them say things they didn't intend to."

"Like vampires." I conclude. He chuckles then agrees, "Yes. Like vampires. That aren't real by the way."

I give him a confused look.

"Aren't vampires one of the four things you're talking about? Vampires, werewolves, zombies and ghosts..." He stops me by shaking his head and laughing.

"No. What gave you that idea?" he asks. I let out an awkward chuckle and shrug. At the same time, he starts to speak.

"There's human or mortal, and when you die you become an angel and go to Heaven, a demon and go to Hell, or a ghost and you're lingering somewhere in-between."

Realisation suddenly hits me, and I start putting up my defenses.

"So, you're really a ghost?" I ask slowly letting go of his hand. He looks down at his empty hand and nods.

"Then, how'd you die?" I whisper. He closes his eyes so he doesn't have to make eye contact or see my reaction.

I know this must be a touchy subject for him, but if I'm going to continue living with him, I'd like to know who or what I'm living with. *If* I decide to stay with him like I said I was going to, but when I had promised him, I wasn't expecting this. This is the reason I wanted to find out before I said yes to anything.

"Walter led everyone to believe that I was the one who had tried to," he pauses, but he doesn't have to finish. I already understand. He was framed. "So they came after me-"

"But why would they think you'd do such a thing?" I interrupt.

"Walter told the kingdom that I must have grown tired of the Duke position and was in dire need of more power." He rolls his eyes and shakes his head, clearly irritated with this Walter character. "And when Walter says 'jump'..."

"Everyone else says 'how high.'" I finish for him. He still isn't looking me in the eyes. He's just staring at the white sheets covering the bed.

"I arrived in London not long after. Eventually, they caught up to me and, that was that." He finally looks up and I get to see all the sadness in his eyes, but there are no tears.

"Gasmine knew how awful and devious her father was. She was by my side every step of the way. She helped me get out of the cellar, you know.

"Once Walter made the accusations and pinned it all on me, I was locked away in the cellar-"

"Like a dungeon?" I ask.

"Yeah," he nods. "Like a dungeon."

"I was sentenced to death, just waiting for the king to decide how: stoning or hanging.

"Gasmine often visited me. But she never got the courage to stand up to her father and tell him that she believes me, not him. She couldn't upset her father. That's just, something she couldn't do.

"I remember her hurrying down the cobblestone steps saying 'you have to leave, now!' and 'you can never come back! Go; get far-far away from here!'

"It turns out, they moved my sentencing to later that evening. She unlocked my cell and shackles, and she led me out a secret gate of some sort. That's how I got to London." I look into his eyes, even though he's desperately trying not to make eye contact. Honestly, I think he just doesn't want me to see the tears brimming in his eyes. I didn't know ghosts- or whatever he is- cried.

He palms his eyes trying to rid himself of all the pain from past memories, but crying is healthy. Even to a ghost, I'm sure. It's supposed to cleanse the soul, even if he doesn't have one.

"Gasmine. She's actually the one I miss seeing everyday." He sniffs the remainder of his tears away and shrugs. He gets up off the bed and just stands there.

"I think it's almost time for me to go..."

"No. Stay. You don't have to go-"

I'm suddenly interrupted by Professor Gates walking in and telling Robbie that visiting hours are almost over. I watch Robbie nod, and head towards the door. Before he leaves, he gives me one last worried glance. Then he shuts the door.

"How are you feeling, Miss Taylor?" Gates folds his hands in his lap as he crosses one leg over the other.

"Alright." I reply. He nods his head and tells me he's planning on calling my parents in the morning.

"Do you really have to? I'm not hurt. I'll be going home tomorrow, can't I call them then?" I ask. I don't want them overreacting. They're way too protective of me. I'm afraid they'd try to take me home and I wouldn't be able to see Robbie anymore.

"That's fine. Maybe it's best you call them." He starts to stand and tells me to get some rest, but once he leaves the room all I can think of is what Robbie had told me. I'm just not sure how I feel about that yet.

ANOTHER THING TO TALK ABOUT.

"And you called them?" Professor Gates asks me for the fourth time in a row.

"Yes, Mr. Gates. I did. They said they put their trust in you completely." Even though I actually hadn't called them, and I wasn't planning to.

"Alright, Miss Taylor." he exhales. "Please be careful, and remember, we re-scheduled for the day after tomorrow. The rain still hasn't let up so please, do stay indoors. You can get back okay?"

I assume he means to Robbie's, so I nod and reply with a simple yes before exiting the hospital doors and getting into a cab to go to Robbie's.

...

I pay the cab driver- it wasn't much- and hustle into the apartment building. The rain is coming down extremely hard though, almost like all day yesterday.

That was terrifying. I'm really glad Robbie was there. Ya know, I don't care if he is a ghost. Or an angel, or a demon for that matter. I haven't known him for that long but, he saved me and that definitely can bring a person closer to another, if anything.

I round the corner to Robbie's apartment, if I remember correctly. 7B.

I knock on the door, but there's no answer. He said he would get me a spare key the other day. He was too busy, I guess. Or maybe he just never got the chance to give it to me.

I reach for the knob and notice it's open. How had I not noticed that before? Why is it open anyway?

I slowly creak open the door the rest of the way and the air feels chilly. Even more so than usual, but there's a ghosts living here, so I guess that's the reason.

That still doesn't explain why the door was open. I mean, if he wanted to leave it unlocked for me he could, but open? I don't think so.

I step inside and close the door behind me. Wandering throughout most of the house- besides the bedroom, I haven't made it there yet- I don't see Robbie.

"Robbie?" I call out his name into the hallway. Hopefully he's in his room, but if not, maybe he's at the bar. I'm not sure why he'd be working. I don't think anyone would want a drink at nine in the morning.

"Robbie?" I knock a couple times and then just decide to enter. I'm getting kind of worried. When I open the door that was keeping me out, my stomach drops and confusion finds its way into my expressions.

It's empty. There is nothing. No bed, no clothes, no Robbie. I guess I'll just wait for him to get back, then I can ask what's going on with the missing furniture in the bedroom. I could get a start on my project that I should be close to finished on, though I'm not.

I close Robbie's door and head into the living room. Taking off my shoulder bag and setting it on the ground, I notice how dusty everything has gotten. In only a day? That doesn't seem right. And the worn out, leather bound journal he used to keep on the coffee table is no longer there either. I'll ask Robbie when he gets home.

I remember finding that thing shoved in between the couch cushions on the second night I stayed here. I flipped through a couple of the pages to find a few poems, what I assumed were thoughts and some random sketches. One of the sentences that I remember most is, 'Sometimes you have to get away to come back stronger.' I don't know why, but that seemed to stick with me.

I take out my notebook and turn to a clean page to jot down some ideas. I find the pencil and label the paper 'topic brainstorming.' I know I already signed up for a topic, but I think I want to choose something in the 'historical people' section instead, and I'm pretty sure I'm doing my project on Robbie. I mean Duke Robert Price.

He did suggest it. If I do remember correctly, he said, "I think this one's an interesting topic. If you want my opinion." And I did want his opinion. It's a very interesting topic. Robbie's very interesting all together.

I can't wait until he gets home. I have so many more questions to ask him. Was this his plan all along? Did he intend for me to be staying with him? Somehow? And at the bookstore. How he had just appeared behind me. I wonder if he really rented that book for me or just pretended to make me feel better. Can a ghost have a library card? Either way, it was sweet.

The way I asked him to join me at the café was strange; it didn't seem like me, and he said so himself, he can make people say things they weren't going to. Did he make me ask him if he wanted to go with me? Something else to talk to him about I guess.

Does Robbie... like me? He's always so nice. Opening doors for me, paying for things. He saved me from Rian, gave me a place to live after and wouldn't let me die. Literally, he pulled me away from death. You wouldn't do that for just anybody. Would you?

Missing ghost.

I suck in a harsh breath and jolt awake. It's freezing. Why does it keep getting colder? I open my eyes and see I fell asleep on the couch.

When I sit up, my pad of paper falls on the ground. It's still blank.

"Dang." I was hoping to have finished it before falling asleep, being able to wake up to a full assignment done and ready to be handed in. Guess that's not how it works.

I lift my lazy-self off the cushions and glance out the window. It's still day, so I couldn't've slept that long. I take my phone out of my bag to check the time, and it reads two-twenty p.m. Wow, quite a while and still no Robbie. Looking around, I see nothing's changed. Maybe the furniture in the apartment has collected a few more dust particles, but that's all.

Where is he? Maybe Professor Gates has heard from him.

I slip my coat back on and leave the apartment, this time with the door shut completely.

...

He wasn't at the college dorms, so hopefully he's here at the hospital.

I enter through the doors and head up to the other students room. You know, I still never found out who that other kid is. Walking through the hall, I see Professor Gates sitting on a waiting chair in front of the door, reading.

As I get closer, he notices my presence and stands. He sets the book aside and asks, "Miss Taylor? Why are you back?"

I finally get in front of him and get the chance to ask.

"You haven't happened to of heard from Robbie, have you?"

He gets this really odd look on his face, almost as if he was confused.

"And who might this Robbie character be? I don't have a student named Robbie in my class."

"No, he's not a student, but you do know him though." I try convincing him, but he just kept shaking his head.

"I'm sorry, Miss Taylor. I don't know who you're talking about." He sits back down and begins to read again.

"Professor Gates. He's the boy that saved me. He's the one I've been staying with-"

"Oh no. That's absurd. Why would I let a student leave campus with someone I don't even know?" he laughs.

"Because, he was my friend. I knew him-"

"How could you possibly know anyone in London?" he interrupts me once again.

"I- I met him at a bookstore-"

"And I just what? Let you live with him for the rest of our stay?" he jokes. "That's irresponsible."

I watch him bend over and pick up where he left off in his book, like I hadn't even interrupted him in the first place.

I head back to the elevators while rolling my eyes. My head's starting to hurt. Where's Robbie and why did Mr. Gates say he didn't know him? I guess the next place to check is the bar.

...

I walk into the entrance and see it's just barely open, and there's almost no one here. I walk up to the bartender who is washing a few glasses.

"Excuse me?" I get his attention.

"What can I get you?" He smiles.

"Oh no. Actually, I'm looking for someone. Robbie? Cunningham? He works here. You know him or seen him?"

He scrunches up his face while he thinks.

"Sorry..." He starts shaking his head.

"Are you sure? Brown, curly hair? About, yay tall?" I lift my hand to show where Robbie's height would be on me. "Ocean blue eyes? Robbie Cunningham? No?"

He just keeps shaking his head.

"There's no one with that name or that fits that description who works here. Sorry."

I rest my head in my hands as I lean on the counter.

"Hey, looks like you've had a rough night." he says.

"You've had no idea..."

"Then how's about I buy you a drink? How does that sound?" he offers.

I smile up at him and take a deep breath.

"No thanks." I say while standing up from my stool.

"Be careful out there." he says while putting a few cups on racks. I nod and start to turn around when he gets my attention again.

"And, I uhh, hope you find your friend." He smiles at me once more, this time without paying attention to something else.

And before walking out the door, I reply, "Me too."

A WALK DOWN MEMORY LANE.

What's another place to look?

The bookstore! He said he hangs out there a lot.

He's probably there and I'm just overreacting. Maybe he's looking up some stuff to help me with my project. He did say he would, you know.

I walk up the steps and to my surprise, it's still unlocked like the first day I came. That means someone's here. Last time it was Robbie. He was the only one here. Hopefully, it'll happen again.

I enter the squeaky door, and it's as though nothing's changed. The bottom of the library area is completely clean and brand new, and from only a quick glance, the top is as dusty as ever.

Without further thought, I begin to wander up the old staircase. That's where he was last time, and I don't see anyone else down here anyways.

"Robbie?" I call out, just about to reach the top. "Are you up here?"

But I get no response, so I continue on my way. Once I'm at the top, I head straight for the section I first met Robbie. Walking down the aisle, I glance over to my left and see the line of books, one in particular catching my eye.

Dive Into History.

The book I was just going to take and leave- return it later- because a certain adorable, cheeky ghost decides to be all creepy and give me weird chills.

I understand more clearly now. Why every spine tingling chill came through, making every hair on my body stand on end. Robbie.

Boy am I glad he did. Otherwise, I would've just ran out with that book and everything would be normal. Did I ever mention how much I hate normal? I don't even think I can remember what "normal" feels like. I don't even want to imagine not meeting Robbie or knowing him.

As I run my fingers along the dust covered spine of the book, I find myself smiling more and more at the thought. How it collected this much dust in a couple of weeks is beyond me, but the memory of how close Robbie was to my backside as he leaned over and gave me his description of the book keeps coming back into my mind.

I can't believe it, but I really miss him. I'm surprised by the effect he's had on me in such a short period of time. Where is that crazy boy? I'm really starting to get worried.

I decide he's not here, but finish my inspection of the place anyway. As I walk down the rest of the aisle, I come across a door in the very back that I don't remember seeing the last time I was here snooping around.

So I enter with curiosity taking the best of me, like it always does.

The room is dark, but the light from the window and the door is just enough for me to see. It's completely empty besides an old, dust covered chest in the corner and a couple dark wooden shelves that have been abandoned.

I kneel down in front of the chest, and see a padlock needing four, two digit numbers. I try a couple made up number combinations before giving up and straightening my back out.

Then I remember Robbie. In my dream he had told me to remember a couple things. Robert Price, and four, two digit number combos. If they'll work on this, I have no idea, but it's worth a try.

I pick up the lock once again, and while wiping off the remainder of dust, I try to recall what exact numbers they were and in what order.

"Okay. Here goes nothin'..." I whisper while turning the dial to twenty six. Then the second to thirty two. Then, forty one, but I can't seem to remember the last number. Twenty one maybe?

I try that, and it doesn't work. So I just start to try random numbers in for the last one. When none of the combinations I've tried works, I let out an annoyed groan. I close my eyes and hold onto the bridge of my nose in frustration.

All of a sudden, I see Robbie, but not like the last couple times he's came to me. It was more like a memory. I saw him on my bed, sitting right beside me.

"...remember. Robert Price..."

As the words began to flow from his mouth, I begin to understand what he's doing. He's giving me the memory of the first time he came to me.

"...twenty six: thirty two: forty one: twelve..."

As those familiar numbers ring throughout my head, I open my eyes and begin turning the dials once again, and this time, it unlocks.

I let out the deep breath I had been holding in, and tilt my head back, whispering into the air.

"Thank you..." I could've sworn, I heard a sweet response saying, 'You're welcome, love. Now don't be shy, rip it open.' But that must've just been in my head because when I look around, Robbie still isn't here.

I feel my shoulders droop from having Robbie absent from my side for so long, but maybe there's something in this chest that will help me find him. Or at least something he wants me to have. Why else would he have given me the combination?

I slide off the lock and slowly open the lid, but no matter how slow I do, dust and everything else will still fly throughout the air.

My eyebrows knit together in confusion as I stare at the one and only item in the center of the otherwise empty chest. A set of keys.

They weren't a normal pair of house keys either. They were old timey, padlock keys. For like a jail cell or something along the same lines.

I pick up the set to inspect them further, and there isn't a speck of dust on them. Which is odd considering the rest of the entire upstairs area is covered in the substance.

As I count the keys- four of them- I wonder what they open. Well, everything leads back to Robbie, so why shouldn't this as well? Meaning, what if the keys go to something of his he had to leave behind in Gloucester.

As I continue to ponder on these keys, I catch a glimpse of something shiny out of the corner of my eye. I take a closer look, and see that it's coming from behind the wooden chest. So I- with all my might- shove it to the right revealing a small-ish door with yet another padlock. I wonder...

I instantly grab a hold of it and try key number one. Nothing. Number two, same.

"This is ridiculous." I say to myself when key three doesn't work either, but when the familiar sound of a lock changing comes from the fourth key turning in the padlock, I grow even more curious.

I- as silently as possible- slide off the lock and chains then look around the almost fully lit room, making sure no one catches me and ends my adventure before it even begins. Plus, I'm not leaving until I find Robbie.

I open the door and see- spider webs to be honest. Thousands of spider webs, but once I move them aside and enter the crawl space on all fours, I see a ledge. A ledge that's overlooking an incredibly creepy hallway.

Just when I start to re-think my previous decision and turn back, I fall face first onto the platform of the ledge. I turn over on my back and grab onto my chin, which I smacked really hard on the concrete when I fell.

"Ow..." I laugh at my own clumsiness and open my eyes. Well no wonder that hurt. I fell from almost seven foot up.

I groan when I realise the fact that there's no way I'm getting back up there.

"So I go down." I say looking over the ledge and onto the hallway. At least it's not too long of a drop. Not as bad as seven feet, that's for sure.

I shrug off the pain, and while still holding onto my chin I land on the concrete in one swift motion. Thank God I wore tennis shoes and jeans today, not my skirt like I was planning.

I remember Robbie telling me he liked that skirt when he was helping me unpack. I thought I'd try to impress him, but then I couldn't find him. So that plan didn't exactly work out.

Two strange voices come booming through the hall making me jump and scurry into a corner to hide.

"What shall I do with the boy, sir?" One man's voice becomes clear and both men come into my view.

"Be-headed! At dawn!" The taller one tells the shorter one.

"And what shall we tell the kingdom, sir?" The short man questions. It's silent for a minute as the tall man thinks.

"Tell them Duke Robert Price is being charged with treason, and we shall have the ceremony at dawn."

"Very well, sir." I hear the smaller man say the last three words as they head in the opposite direction from which they came.

Now I know what I'm supposed to do.

I have to find Robbie.

Him.

I've been wandering for what feels like hours. My cell phone stopped working for some strange reason. It's been eight-twenty five p.m. since I checked the first time. So I'm positive the clocks not working.

After those men were out of sight, I decided to go down the hall they came from and I came to a four way crossing.

When I went down the hall on the left, it took me to a bunch of rooms, but they were all fancy like a dining hall or a music room, not a dungeon; I'm sure that's where Robbie is.

The one I'm on now is just a hall with wonderful décor and paintings. The people in the paintings all have on fancy old clothes. They have amazing headdresses and some of them even wore armor.

Then I come across a picture that somewhat looks like Robbie. His hair is slicked back. Even so, a few curls had gotten free. He's wearing armor on his chest and he's holding a helmet in his left hand, sword in his right.

Although, his bottom half is covered in this weird form fitting grey pants and boots. I must admit, he looks good, and happy.

The smile on his face is so genuine and sincere. I don't understand why anyone would want to hurt this adorable boy.

He looks younger. I notice the plaque at the bottom of the painting that reads 'Duke Robert Price, 1750.'

He said he was crowned at sixteen, but it took a few years to train and be given the honor of Duke. I'm guessing he's about eighteen here. Around my age.

I quickly take out my almost useless phone and snap a picture of the painting on the wall. I can't believe how handsome he is.

I really have to find him.

...

The last hallway leads me down some stairs. The floors and walls are concrete and stone, definitely not home decorated like the other halls. So this must be it. I walk further down the hall and it just keeps getting darker, less light and less windows.

I check my pocket to make sure that I still have the keys, and I do. Then I come across an opening and I stop.

I glance around and behind me to make sure no one's coming. Then I start checking every locked door. When one finally opens, I enter and see many cells.

I slowly walk past them one at a time and peek inside. Most of them are empty. Until I come across a cell on the left that contains a man that looks to be in his mid-thirties.

He notices me and jumps up from his bench. The closer he gets, the farther I back away, but every time he comes towards me he gets jerked back by the chains around his ankles.

"Fair maiden?" he speaks as he grips the bars that are keeping us apart.

I take a step closer when I figure he can't touch me.

"Would you be ever so kind as to hand me those keys?" His deep accent is almost similar to Robbie's.

He points to the keys in my hand. I look down at them and he says, "Yes, love. Those. Give em' here..."

He waves for me to place them in his hand, but I need them for Robbie. So I ignore him and continue down the hall, but I can still hear him shouting for me to come back.

The farther I walk, the more empty cells I see. There's only a couple left to check. Then I see there's someone in the second to last cell. It's a boy sitting on a bench behind the bars. All I can really make out are his dark brown curls atop his head, but even then I knew it was him. It was Robbie.

I hurry over to the bars trying to be quiet, but I end up making a lot of noise actually, and it gets Robbie's attention.

His head tilts up and then forward. When he spots me, his eyes light up as he stands.

"You made it!" he says grasping onto the brass.

I take a deep breath and nod. For some reason, I can't find any words to say. A simple 'yeah I did' would've been fine, but just seeing him this way... His hair's all messed up- worse than usual- and he has cuts and scrapes all over his face. Yet, he still manages to smile.

I lift up my hand and jingle the keys in front of the lock. I watch a giant smile form on his face as he starts to speak again.

"I knew I could count on you, love. Now open it and try to be quick." I bend down and start to unlock the cell door.

The fourth key went to the weird crawl space door, so it's not that one. I try the first one, it doesn't work.

"Try the odd shaped one." Robbie says still watching me.

"They're all odd shaped to me!" I say getting a bit stressed. I think I feel a headache coming on.

I hear Robbie let out a short chuckle and say, "Try the third one, doll."

I glance up and he still had that addictive, sassy smile on his face.

I do as I'm told and the gate slides open when Robbie gives it a small push. Then he gets jerked back because of the chains attached to the wall and his leg.

"Are you alright?" I rush over to his side and kneel down. He reaches up and rubs the back of his head that hit the bench as he fell.

"Just lovely..." he groans. "Get the bloody shackles off, would you?"

"Right..." I reach over to his ankles and see how tight they were on him. There's a gaping hole in his blue jeans on the right side, and I can see cuts and bruises all over his leg.

"Do hurry." he says while keeping a watch down the hall.

As I unlock one leg, then the other, I was careful not to hurt him any further. He probably couldn't take anymore. I know I couldn't if I was even half as banged up as him.

"Thank you!" I was suddenly being pulled into a giant bear hug by Robbie when the last of his chains were unlocked and he was free.

"Thank you so much, love. You're absolutely amazing." I feel him run his fingers through my hair as he whispers to me. "I owe you, and I trust you with my life completely."

I pull him back at arm's length, and give him a weird look because he referred to himself as having a life while being a ghost. He rolls his eyes when he finally catches on and says, "You know what I mean."

I laugh and he grabs ahold of my hand.

"How could I ever repay you?" I look down to our intertwined fingers, then up to his eyes. Even though his entire body looks as though he's in seriously bad shape, his eyes are still as blue as ever.

"You can start by showing me a way out of here. Wherever here is." I say while helping him to his feet.

He chuckles and says, "You're in Gloucester."

"I figured that." I say draping his arms around my shoulders. Poor thing hurt his leg so bad, all he could do is stumble. "But I was just in London. How am I in Gloucester?"

We start to head down the hall with Robbie hopping on his good side, me carrying his excess weight.

"Well, you must of used the small wooden door in the bookstore? That's the last place I was able to see you. Due to the fact, I'm not exactly a ghost here." I nod as we continue down the hall.

"*He* set that up so he could keep an eye on me. He made it to where if he wanted to, he could bring me back if I messed up..."

"Wait. Who's *He*?" I try to ask, but I get cut off when we walk past that man from earlier's cell.

"Duke Price! Duke Price!" He tries to get Robbie's attention. I watch Robbie glare at him as we slowed to a stop.

"Be a mate and hand me those keys the lovely maiden has in her hand."

"Ignore him..." Robbie says as we continue down the hall, this time at a faster pace. I decide to let the *He* thing go until I know we're safe and in present time London, not past time Gloucester. The entire time we've been walking, Robbie's been groaning in pain.

"Are you okay? Do you have to stop?" I ask.

He shakes his head and says, "The sooner we reach the bookstore, the better."

I nod and we slowly come across the ledge. It looks even higher up than when I was here before.

"This is it?" he asks while removing his arm from my shoulder. To be honest, I kind of missed it.

"Uh huh." I agree to his assumption while staring up at what seemed to be the only exit. I look over and see Robbie wobbling around the ledge trying to find a way up.

"Robbie, there's no way up."

"There has to be something." he says as he continues to hop around on his good leg. All of a sudden, I start feeling light headed, and that headache was growing stronger by the second.

I get a head rush and take to my knees while slamming my hand to my forehead.

"Carolina?" Robbie says while rushing to my side. I feel him place his hand on either sides of my face while tilting my head up to look at him.

"Carolina... stay with me..." His voice starts getting quieter and his image is getting blurry. The last thing I remember was dropping the keys, and falling backwards into Robbie's arms as he gently eased me to the ground, babbling something about *Him* taking me.

A LIFE FOR A LIFE.

I feel a change occurring, and it's showing. My skin looks as clear as water, almost see through. A million little blue vines were coming into view as it rushes through my veins.

"What are you doing to her?"

My entire body grew whiter and whiter by the second.

"Stop! She was only trying to help!"

A flood of emotions start to hit me. Guilt, anger, love, fear. All at once, it's hitting my chest, and then it stops.

I fall limp to the concrete and my breathing ceases. I feel what's left of my breath go cold and my mouth dry. I no longer had the strength to hold my head up. So I lie there. Just, lie there.

My eyelids drape shut as I hear another voice.

"You wanted this! You asked for this! There's no going back now..."

Robbie's POV:

I watch as Carolina falls to the ground right in front of me.

"You wanted this! You asked for this! There's no going back now..." I watch *Him* squeeze his hand shut fully, causing Carolina to yell in pain.

I kneel down beside her and just watch. I know there's nothing I can do to save her. I tuck a strand of hair behind her ear and turn to him.

"That's not what I meant by let me be with her and you know it!"

"Fine! You want her? What are you willing to give up for her?" By the look in his eyes, I knew what he wanted.

"You want me to join you?" I ask while grabbing Carolina's almost lifeless hand.

"I want you to move on. It's for the best. Do you honestly believe she loves you? You're a lost soul, Robert. She's mortal. Sooner or later, you'll have to make this decision. I'm trying to help you make it now before you get into something that's obviously not logical." *He* unclenches his hand and tells me to choose. "You're life, or her's?"

I glance down at her and see her almost white skin slowly turn pink again.

"I'm a ghost remember. I don't have a life."

"But you could. If you join me-"

"So you do want me to join you?" I question.

"If we're getting technical. But isn't this what you want? Immortal life? To never be harmed. To be taken off the radar?" he asks.

"I told you I didn't care about that anymore-"

"Of course you do! That's the entire reason you chose her! She was the only one who could help you. And now. I'm the only one that can help you."

I start to shake my head and tell him no. When I agreed to this earlier, before I met Carolina, I was promised life as an angel, not a demon. And this man right here, would become my master if I agreed to become almost everybody's nightmare.

"No. I will not join your, cult!" *He* starts to laugh and it shakes the entire ground.

"Cult is an understatement. Almost 3/5 of the earth's population are mine. My creatures have been roaming the earth, terrorizing mortals for centuries. And there are more underground. Waiting to get the honor, to be in my "cult"."

"How many more?" I ask while standing on my good foot.

"Thousands." He raises his hands up indicating how powerful he is. "And the numbers are only growing."

I look back to Carolina who still hasn't moved, but is already looking better.

"Then you shouldn't need me." I start to turn and hop back to her when he stops me.

"It's not that I need you. It's that I want you. Robert, I can help you." The sharp pain I used to feel in my leg is suddenly gone and so are the cuts on my face.

I vastly turn my head towards him and see his hands in the air. A smile on his face.

"Tell you what. You come with me now and in return, I'll restore her breath..." *He* breathes into his closed fist and when he opens it, a small cloud starts forming in the palm of his hand.

"But if you don't," *He* crushes the cloud and I see three tall men dressed in black suits with evil smiles plastered on their faces walk out from behind him and pass me, heading to Carolina. "I'll have my men take her body away. And I'll make sure you stay a ghost until the end of time. No loopholes, no deals, no second chances."

I start shaking my head and hear him say, "Very well then."

He waves his hand to the men and they begin picking up Carolina. "Wait!"

He turns back around and smiles.

"Glad you came to your senses."

A NEW BEGINNING.

"Carolina. You're still not out of bed? I told you to get up an hour ago. You're gonna be late!" I hear a man's voice. Then something hits my backside.

"Hey!" I turn around and open my eyes to see Rian standing above me fastening his belt.

"Oh come on. Like you've never let me touch you there before." He smiles and tells me to get dressed.

"Big day today. Saying goodbye to England." He opens the closet and pulls out a pair of my jean shorts and a tank top. "It's supposed to be hot."

He winks and tosses the articles of clothing onto my lap. I sit up in bed and palm my eyes, taking away the rest of my sleep.

I look up and see Rian has disappeared into the bathroom, shortly returning with a toothbrush hanging from his mouth.

"Come on, babe. Get dressed." he mumbles accidentally dripping foam all over his clean shirt.

He turns to the closet mumbling something under his breath and takes off the article of clothing to change.

"You know... I had that dream again." I say trying to start up a conversation while changing into my shorts.

"About that blue eyed fellow?" he questions while tossing me a clean bra.

"Yeah."

He hums in confusion and goes back to the bathroom. I quickly change into my bra and tank top before he returns. He walks over and sits down at my bedside.

"You've been having that same dream since we've arrived." he states.

"I know…" I have been, and it's quite scary. It's like I knew him. Although, I don't. I've never met a boy with baby blue eyes, curly brown locks and a sweet smile with dimples embedded deep into the center of his cheeks. "Do you think it means something?"

Rian puts on his thinking face and grabs my hand.

"Probably not. This dude is just a figure in your imagination. Just someone you made up in your head. It's nothing…" he pauses to smile at me. "Now, don't you worry about it. I don't want you to make wrinkles on your perfect little forehead."

He tilts my head down and leaves a soft kiss above my nose, right in between my eyebrows.

"Or ya know, maybe he's my dream guy." I wiggle my eyebrows at him and his smile turns into a frown.

"Then what does that make me?" he pouts.

"Hmm… my boy toy?" I state, in the form of a question. He rolls his eyes and starts to stand, but I pull him back down.

"Come on, dear. I'm just kidding. That makes you my boyfriend. Nothing's changed from the first day we've got here till now. I could have that dream, every day of my life. Doesn't mean I'll fall in love with the blue eyed boy and dump you. Cause guess what?" I pause to see his reaction.

When he doesn't move, or even break eye contact by blinking I continue.

"I love you, way more than some stupid figment of my imagination."

"So you don't think that in your mind, that's the kind of guy you're waiting for?" he questions.

I smile and shake my head.

"I couldn't come up with something more perfect than the boy sitting in front of me right now." I lean in connecting our lips before going to finish getting ready.

I really am lucky to be with such an amazing boy.

FIRST CHARGE.

"The bus is leaving at five p.m. to the airport. I want everyone to be sure to be back here by four-thirty. Understand?" Professor Gates instructs.

"Alright." he smiles. "Go enjoy your last day."

Almost all of the students start to cheer and separate, besides me, Rian and a group of his friends.

"Where are we gonna eat?" one of the taller guys in the huddle asks. I feel Rian grab my hand as we start listening to the other boys.

"Sam. We just ate breakfast before we left." one of them says.

"Okay. Then how about lunch?" Sam asks.

"It's not even ten." Rian speaks up.

"Fine, brunch?" Everyone laughs. This guy must eat a lot for a skinny guy like him. While they continue to talk, I start to look around wondering where it is I want to go on my last day. I actually really want to see Big Ben. You can't go to London and not see it.

There are so many people around. Most of them have cameras, so I'm assuming tourists. If we want to see anything, we shouldn't just be standing here and talking.

Then someone catches my eye. A boy not too far away. He somewhat resembles the boy I've had dreams about for the past month I've been here in London.

He looks exactly like him- from what I can see- but he seems to be dressed differently. Instead of wearing colorful shirts and bottoms, he's dressed in all black. Black jeans and a tight black muscle T showing off his almost tattoo sleeves.

His hair is styled differently too. Still dark brown and curly, but instead of having the curls go free, they were tamed and wrapped behind a bandana. He's much tanner as well. In my dreams he looked white. Almost ghost like. Now, he's got a golden glow. Almost like he got burnt.

I back up from the group a bit to get a better look at the boy. He's just standing there across the walkway. His hands are behind his back as he watches people walk by.

When he notices me watching him, his arms drop and he looks scared. His eyes grow to the size of quarters as he quickly turns on his heels and heads through the park to escape.

I start to turn and follow him, but my hand is still tightly wound in Rians.

"Where are you goin', babe?" he asks.

"I'll just be right back." I say without taking my eyes off of the boy, slowly growing smaller by the second. I hear Rian say okay, but I didn't stop to explain why. I was already headed to the park to find the boy from my dream.

...

I think I lost him. I was chasing after him at first, but once I caught up, I decided to just follow him. I don't think he knew because he slowed his pace, which is good, but I definitely lost him.

He was just here, but when he walked behind this tree, he vanished. I've searched all around this big oak tree, even in it- as if he climbed- but he completely disappeared.

Although, I did find out exactly what he looks like. Just as I thought, eyes that were blue and dimples. He looks exactly like the boy from my dream, just an older version. I jump when I feel a hand on my shoulder, but when I turn around, I see it's only Rian.

"Gosh. You scared me!" I go to slap him lightly on the chest, but he catches it.

"I've been looking everywhere for you. Don't run off without telling me where you're going." He places his free hand on my cheek and smiles down at me. "I don't want to lose you."

"I'm not going anywhere." I smile back up at him as he rests his forehead on mine.

"Yes. But you don't know how many freaks there are out there." he argues.

"Oh blah blah blah..." I push him away and start heading back towards where I last saw the group of Rians friends. He catches up to me and sneaks his arm around my waist.

"We'll be meeting everyone at the diner around eleven-thirty for lunch. Until then, where do you want to go?" he asks.

"Big Ben!"

Robbie's POV:

"She saw you?"

I nod in agreement.

"That's what I said!" I run my hands over the nape of my neck as I wait for my newest friend- really my only friend down here- to give me his opinion. I hear him exhale.

"That's not good, Robbie. *He's* gonna kill you..."

"You're probably right. But James, I don't think you understand." I turn towards the red haired boy. "When she looked at me, I swear... She remembers me-"

"That's where *you* don't understand, Robbie. *He* erased her memory so that she could continue to live. Not so you could follow her around and meet her for the first time, all over again." He rolls his eyes and gets in the project line.

Every month, every demon is assigned a charge. Usually a mortal. This upcoming month will be my first, considering the fact that I'm new at this, but James, he tells me he's been down here for longer than he can even remember.

"So are you excited to get your first charge?" James nudges my shoulder as we move forward in the line.

"Yeah." I smile, but in all reality, I'm terrified. I know this isn't right. Even James knows it's not right. He just doesn't care. We shouldn't go up to torture innocent people.

"You're still nervous, aren't you?" he assumes. "Don't worry. Once you collect this fear, you'll grow stronger. Pretty soon, you won't be able to feel the guilt for your charge."

"Maybe I don't want to give it all up. We shouldn't be tormenting people like this. It's not right."

"Awe, Robbie still has a conscience." he laughs. "Don't worry. That'll be gone soon too."

I'm actually afraid for it all to go away, but *He* said that in order for me to live forever, I have to be drained from all the things helping me hold onto the past. Whether it be my emotions, my memories, or her, they have to go.

It's a process. That's why it's taking so long. In order for it to disappear completely, I have to get stronger. Therefore, the charges.

We're supposed to stalk these people, get inside their heads, and become their worst nightmare. It's like we feast off their fear. The fear, is what keeps us alive.

I'm not sure what keeps the angels alive, but I know they're able to keep everything from previous lives. So I'm not sure why we can't.

"James. Back again?" The lady in the black suit behind the counter reaches into a bin and pulls out two files.

"Yeah." he agrees.

"What does this make? Six this month?" she asks while typing something into a computer.

I look to James and he nods proudly. Him and a couple others are trying to see who can get the most in a month.

"Yes ma'am. And I brought newbie with me." He looks towards me. She glances across the counter at me and smiles.

"I can tell, he'll do nicely." She hands us the file folders and says, "Enjoy these. And, welcome to the pack Robbie."

I don't know how she knew my name, but I said thanks anyway. We turn to leave, but James stops me. He starts laughing while staring into the file the lady handed him.

"Looks like I got your forbidden lover." he jokes.

I yank the folder from his hands and look at it. The first thing I see is a photo of Carolina, then all her information.

"You got Carolina's file!?"

IN ALL BLACK.

Carolina's POV:

"Isn't London magnificent?" I ask while holding onto Rian's hand tightly.

"Whoa, babe. Don't squeeze so hard." he laughs, so I loosen my grip.

"Sorry." I look to the side of the bus and see all of the people below on the streets. I am so happy I don't have anywhere I really have to be until four-thirty. They all look like they're in a hurry. Not me.

I smile at the thought and Rian notices.

"What are you so cheery about all of a sudden?" I glance up at him and shrug, still with that smile on my face.

The bus comes to a complete stop, and Rian and I were the only ones on the top level to stand.

"There must be some reason?" he asks while helping me down off the bus steps.

"Nothing really. Just happy to be here with you is all." He smiles down to me as we walk along the sidewalk. Then he pulls me to a stop.

He grasps my hands in his and leans down to leave a short kiss on my lips.

"How did I ever get so lucky?" he whispers. Then connects our lips again.

"Who's the real lucky one here?" I ask. He chuckles and went to leave a small kiss on the tip of my nose, but when he starts to pull away, his head comes back down and knocks into the side of mine.

"Hey! Watch it!" He turns and faces some dude that was behind him. The guy is smiling.

"Hey, bro. Maybe you should uh, suck face somewhere else. This is a sidewalk. I'm tryna walk here." The boy looks at me and winks, then tries continuing down the walkway, but Rian places his hand against the guy's chest and pushes him back.

"Whoa. Dude, it's all cool. I'll let you get back to your uh, lovely girlfriend back there." He leans past Rian and smiles at me.

"Back off man." Rian warns. You can tell that now, he's mad. His voice got deeper and he was speaking through clenched teeth.

"Alright, sorry. Here. Maybe we got off on the wrong foot. Let me introduce myself. I'm James." He holds out his hand to Rian, but he just stares at it.

"Okay..." James pulls his hand back and runs it through his bright orange hair. "I guess I'll see you guys 'round."

He smiles at Rian then turns to me.

"Bye Carolina." Then he was gone, heading in the opposite direction he was coming from when he bumped into us.

"Who was that and how'd he know your name?" Rian asks. I was just asking myself that same question.

"I don't know. I've never seen him before." He nods and his features soften.

"Are you okay?" he asks while inspecting my forehead to make sure I wasn't bleeding or anything.

"I'm fine. Let's just head to the diner." He agrees, and we start walking hand in hand to the restaurant.

But I couldn't keep my mind off that guy. He was dressed just like the boy from my dream. In all black.

Just trade me.

Robbie's POV:

I haven't even looked at my own file yet. I'm too busy trying to find James. I can't let him hurt Carolina.

All of a sudden, I see him strolling towards me with his hands in his jeans and a satisfied smile on his face.

"Still following me? Huh, Robert?" He just casually walks past me, causing me to turn on my heels and catch up.

"I'd stop if you'd just trade me." I try handing him my file.

"Mmm... nah. This project is going to be fun." he laughs. "She's really somethin' isn't she?"

He smiles at me, and I can tell he's just trying to get under my skin.

"She really means a lot to me, mate. Please?" I start begging.

"Face it Robbie. You're a demon now, and she's forgotten all about you. And now, she's my charge. What would you do with her anyhow?" he asks while kicking a rock across the sidewalk.

"I just don't want her to get hurt. I guess I'd-"

"Keep her safe?" he finishes for me and I nod.

"Well, news flash Robbie. She'll never be safe. If you didn't have her, and I didn't have her, somebody else would. You can't keep a charge their entire life. We alternate and that's the way it works." He picks up the rock and chucks it into a nearby pond.

"Yeah, but maybe somehow I could-"

"Robbie. I'm doing you a favor. Would you rather have her assigned to me, or some psycho newbie- like yourself- who's getting a taste of fear for the first time? It's like a drug, Robbie. They're gonna enjoy it." I start to speak, but he interrupts me again.

"And hopefully this can help you too. It'll give you some closure. You'll finally get over her. Whatever happened between you two in the past is gone. Just focus on your charge, and let me focus on mine." he laughs.

"James-"

"Look, Robbie. I'll even go easy on her for you, okay? She'll be safe with me, alright?" I roll my eyes as he continues. "Well, she'll probably be scared out of her mind and never sleep again. But she'll be safe, enough."

"Are you kidding?" I ask, scared for Carolina.

"Of course I'm kidding... for the most part. But that's not the point. Just get through this first charge," he points to the folder in my hand. "And your mind will be preoccupied with gaining strength, you won't even be worried about how she's doing or where she's at. You'll forget about her, the way she forgot about you."

Carolina's POV:

Who was that?

I think to myself while sucking down the rest of my drink.

"Whoa, Carolina. Slow down a bit. You're gonna get sick." Rian jokes while taking a drink himself.

"Sorry. I'm just nervous." I get this way when I'm worried.

"About?" he asks.

Should I tell him about seeing and following that boy from my dream? Then the boy and knowing me? Calling me by my name.

"I saw him." I start, slowly feeling my heartbeat grow in speed just thinking of him.

"Saw who, babe?" He grabs my hand.

"The boy with blue eyes." He gives me a really weird look, so I continue. "I actually followed him earlier through the park. When I left?"

He nods indicating he understands.

"I saw him standing there. Watching. And when he saw me, he started to run away, but I followed him, until he disappeared." I stop when he lets go of my hand and starts shaking his head.

"You don't believe me?" I ask. He shakes his head again and says, "I don't know what you think you saw, but your dream is not coming to life. You didn't see that same boy. You probably just accidentally stalked someone who looked like him."

"I didn't stalk him. And it was him. I know that face. I see it every night." I'm starting to get overwhelmed. He doesn't believe me.

"Shh, don't raise your voice. Just calm down. Let's not make a scene. It's really not that important, is it?" He holds his head up and looks around to make sure the volume of my voice hadn't disturbed anyone. Even though, it wasn't that loud.

But I agreed anyway, choosing to let it go.

"No. I guess you're right..."

"Good. So where are the guys? It's already twelve." He checks his watch and glances out the window. I shrug. How am I supposed to know? They're his friends, not mine.

"Babe. Don't get upset. I didn't mean it like that. It's just not possible. That's all." He tries to sugar coat it, but all I want to do is forget about it.

Rian's been kind of a jerk lately.

SAFER.

Robbie's POV:

I can't seem to focus on my charge knowing James has Carolina as an assignment, and James never "goes easy". The things he could and probably will do to her, sicken me.

So I put my own assignment on hold, and instead of following James this time, I'm following Carolina, and she is with none other than Rian. That stupid wanker I was forced to leave her with.

He even made me come up with new memories that include only them to replace the ones that involve me. Because, 'erasing their minds is not enough'. I think they've done enough.

Right now, they're in a café eating and laughing, and it sends pains throughout my chest. Which I don't exactly mind at the moment because it just lets me know that I can still feel, and if I can feel, I still have a heart.

If I have that, I still have a chance.

Carolina's POV:

"But that girl is terrible at her job." Rian says so loudly he's almost shouting. I shush him and tell him not to be so loud.

"Why?" he snaps.

"Because, that's rude. We're in public." I reply.

"I don't care. She's awful." he says while taking a giant bite of his sandwich. Currently, he's ranting about our waitress.

"She won't be getting a tip from me." He's talking with his mouthful. I roll my eyes and try to finish my plate.

...

"Come on. Let's get out of here, they have awful service. And the food wasn't even that good... " Rian's voice trails off as he starts for the door.

I don't know what he's talking about. My food was great and the service wasn't that bad. It was just a little slower than he would have liked it to have been.

I look down at the bill and see the stack of money Rian had left with no tip, just like he said. I reach into my wallet and pull out a few more bills for the waitress. I was just about to lay them down when Rian's voice scares me.

"What do you think you're doing?"

Robbie's POV:

I watch as Carolina jumps when Rian appears behind her. I figure he just accidentally startled her, but when Rian snatches her up off the booth by her arm and whispers something in her ear, I know she did something he didn't like.

I walk closer to the shop and realise no one notices him holding onto her like that. I see Carolina make a face like she's in pain when Rian grabs onto her fist with his other hand.

He continues speaking into her ear and finally gets her to release whatever is it that was wrapped up so tightly in her hand. He holds up the item and starts talking about it causing Carolina to close her eyes. When I look closer, I see a couple bills in his fist. Then he shoves them into his pocket.

Money? He's hurting her over money! I feel my hands clench together and before I knew it, I was already across the street about to enter the shop.

I stop in my tracks to try and calm down.

She'll be fine, I think to myself.

"Just fine..." I repeat out loud and back away from the door. I can't just walk up and help her like I had before. She doesn't know me now. She doesn't remember.

I can't just appear and force her back into my life. As wrong as it seems, she'll be safer with Rian than she ever could with me.

I slowly back away, but not forever. I'll be back, but then, I'll be in the shadows where I can protect her from a distance.

Where I can protect her from James.

MADE MY PEACE.

Carolina's POV:

I glance at the mark on my right arm, just above the elbow. Rian's been acting like this lately. Dominating. I'm not sure why.

Back at the diner he caught me leaving a tip and took back the money. I can still hear his raspy voice whispering in my ear and I can still feel his breath running down my neck.

'Didn't I tell you we weren't leaving a tip?'

Nobody even tried standing up to him, like what he was doing was normal. Except this lady in the corner with coffee. She saw the entire thing but did nothing. We made eye contact a couple of times, still nothing. She'd just get scared and look back to her book.

I'm just happy it's over, and hopefully he won't do it again. He hasn't been speaking to me for a while. He's just dragging me around to places he wants to see. All of a sudden, he wraps his arms around my waist and lays his chin on my shoulder.

"I'm sorry, babe." he whispers into my ear.

"I don't want to fight. I didn't mean to scare you like that." He pauses for me to speak, but I'm afraid to.

"Aren't you gonna say something?" he says kind of rough. I wait for a minute then ask, "Can I?"

Which causes a deep chuckle to force its way up Rian's chest.

"Of course, babe." He leaves a kiss on the side of my neck.

"I'm sorry too..." I tell him what I think he wants to hear.

"For?" he presses on as we look up at the tall building in front of us. "For trying to leave a tip when you didn't want to."

He kisses my cheek and says, "Good girl."

As we start walking down the sidewalk, I keep getting this awkward feeling that someone is following us. So every once in awhile I'll turn around. Rian got mad at me a couple times but I couldn't sketch the feeling.

"Carolina! Stop!" he says pulling my hand forward.

"I'm sorry. I thought I saw someone..."

"There are people all around you, Carolina. I would hope you see at least someone." he snaps, jerking me forward again and into his side.

I'm afraid to say anything else so I just stay by his side and stay quiet.

Robbie's POV:

I want to just walk up to them, punch Rian in the throat and take Carolina with me. She might not be as safe with me due to what I am now, but I know for a fact I wouldn't be the one hurting her.

He said no loopholes, deals or second chances, but there has to be something. I don't want to be a demon but I've made my peace with it, but I cannot make my peace with this. If Rian hurts her one more time, I'm not sure I'll be able to control myself.

FOLLOWING THE TARGET.

"I'm working on my sixth!" James continues to brag about his charge.

"And she's an interesting one." He turns back and winks at me.

"And your status report?" the Head Chair asks.

"Great. I "ran" into her and her boyfriend earlier. Right after I picked a fight with the boy, I called her by her name and just left. She'll definitely be thinking about me for a while." He takes his seat next to me and the Head Chair starts to speak.

"Fantastic! That's a great beginners move. Get inside their head and make them wonder, Who is that? How did he know me? Will I see him again? Classic." Everyone around the 'field report group' agrees. Except me.

"What advice would you give other beginners such as Zack or Robbie?" he mentions my name and my head shoots over to James. He had a smug look on his face.

"I guess I'd say don't worry too much about this first charge. You'll get used to the feeling." He turns to look at me then continues. "Practice makes perfect. So don't sweat it."

"Alright. Nice advice. Robbie, how's your first charge coming along?" It's my turn to share with my experience.

"I have yet to choose my first move..." I whisper.

"That's fine. Take your time, but remember what James said. Don't worry too much on this first one. It's best to get it done and over with. Collect your bounty and move on."

I glance over at James and he's nodding as if to say I told you so. Then an idea pops into my head.

"Head Chair? I have an idea on what to do with this charge, I just might need someone with as much experience as James to coach me." I look to James and he's confused.

"What are you up to?" he whispers to me, but I was already trying to focus on the Head Chair.

"Something extravagant?" he asks. I nod and he tells me that's great. "Show up these hot shots who think they're too good to be on our level. James, you'll help him."

He starts to move on after James and I were dismissed. As soon as we step into the hall, I'm shoved backwards.

"You idiot!" James grabs onto my collar tightly and screams at me. "What was that?"

I stare deep into the pool of black that has become his eyes. By the look on his face, you'd think I'd be scared, but all I could do was smile.

Carolina's POV:

"Everyone on!" Professor Gates loads students onto the bus to the airport. I'm really not ready to leave and I keep feeling as though I'm forgetting something.

"Hey. When we get off the plane stay near the gate, alright? I'll pick you up there." Rian instructs. I nod and silently thank God that I don't have to ride home with Rian by my side. I don't know who I'm sitting with, but it's alright.

As long as it's not Rian.

Robbie's POV:

"Wuss!" James finally lets go of me after I tell him my plan and starts to head in the other direction. "Now I won't have enough time for my own charge."

"Good. Carolina should be safe that way-"

116

"I don't even care about your girl. I wanna win that bet!" he snaps.

"You wanna know what? Forget you, two can play at that game..."
With that, he turns and heads towards the 'field report group' room. So I follow him.

He steps inside for a while then reappears with a huge smile on his face. I start to ask what he's up to when he interrupts me.

"You want my coaching? I'll give you my coaching. Come on." He tugs me towards the exit which also happened to lead up to the mortal world.

"Where are we going?" I ask.

"Tennessee."

PROOF.

Carolina's POV:

I hope it stays like this. I'm at the window seat and I hope the other two seats stay empty. I'd love to have this time to myself.

As soon as I plug up my headphones, my eyes drape shut and I begin to rest. I place some gum in my mouth and start crumbling the wrapper between my fingers.

"Can I have piece?" I hear a quiet voice, even though the music's blaring in my ears. It kind of sounds like...

I open my eyes to find the red haired boy that knew my name beside me. As I unplug one of my headphones and stare at him in disbelief, he starts to speak.

"Hey..." he says recognising me. I feel my stomach drop inside. Something about this boy gives me a strange, unsettling feeling, and how he's connected to the blue eyed boy scares me even more.

"Aren't you gonna say hi?" he whispers while leaning over to my side making shivers go down my spine. I don't like the feeling this guy gives me.

"Hello?" I reply trying not to make too much eye contact. For a few minutes he just stares at me so I decide to hand him the piece of gum he asked for earlier.

"Thanks." he says shoving the stick in his mouth. "What about my uh, friend over here?"

He points over to the other chair in the small section, but instead of being empty like before, it's occupied. I lean forward to get a good look at the boy but he's resting his chin in the palm of his hand, somewhat hiding his face.

"Hey... want some gum?" The red haired boy nudges him and he peeks out from behind his hand. Almost like he didn't want to be seen. He looks directly at me with a mixed emotion of guilt, pity and worry. Then I realise.

Tight black jeans, form fitting black T and black tattoos to match. Dark brown curls behind a green camouflage bandana. Dimples I could barely make out at the cause of worry and dark, deep ocean blue eyes.

I know what I saw, and what I saw is right here in front of me.

THAT'S ME.

"No... I'm good." he speaks. His piercing blue eyes never losing contact with mine. Until I look away and to the window.

I'm staring at the afternoon sky and how all the clouds below are so full and white. They're nothing compared to the thoughts clouding up my mind. Dark, stormy thoughts about the red haired boy, Rian, and the blue eyed boy from my dream.

"Hate to bother you again..." I look towards him and the other boy is facing the other direction, once again hiding. "Where is this plane headed? Do you know?"

I give him a confused look. Why would he be on the plane if he didn't know where it's going?

"Tennessee." I answer. I turn back towards the window to ignore the boy but something he says brings me back.

"Thanks, Taylor."

"What did you call me?" I reposition myself to be facing him.

He smiles and repeats, "Taylor?"

"How do you know my name? And my nickname?" I ask in a whisper. It might not be the best idea, but I already said it. He turns towards the blue eyed boy, who is now watching intently.

"We both know you. Right, Robbie?" The boy's blue eyes grow at the sound of his name. He opens his mouth to speak but nothing comes out.

"Don't mind him." He turns back to me. "Whenever he's around a girl as stunning as yourself, it's like a cat's got his tongue."

He laughs at the boy named Robbie then introduces himself.

"I'm James by the way. And that's Robbie, if you haven't figured that out." I don't know what to say with both of them watching me. It's making me nervous and I feel like I'm going to pass out.

"Heading home then?" James asks sitting back giving me a better view of Robbie.

As James crosses one leg over the other I reply, "How would you know that?"

My eyes go from his to Robbie's as James let out a few short chuckles. Robbie seems to be waiting for James' answer as well.

"Well you're not English. So I assumed." I roll my eyes at my own stupidity and force up a smile.

"Are you heading home as well?" I decide to ask. Hopefully being friendly will hide the fact that I'm scared out of my mind, and that this guy is the cause of it.

"Nah. I'm from Florida. Haven't been there in centuries though." He looks to Robbie as Robbie rolls his eyes at the comment. I'm guessing an inside joke of some sort.

"And you?" I say getting Robbie's attention. I honestly don't care too much about James. I want to know about the blue eyed boy from my dream. He looks scared to speak at first.

"No. I'm from uh, Gloucester. Originally."

"Gloucester?" I ask. Something about the name is familiar. I think it was in my dream as well.

"Yeah. You ever been?" James asks. At first I thought about it. I feel like I have but, the only place in England- or anywhere besides Tennessee- I've been to is London.

"No. I haven't." I reach into my carry on shoulder bag and grab out my notebook. I open up to the page I started jotting down ideas on the other night in the dorm. I don't have many.

Glancing through the list, I'm stumped. I have a week before it's due. I had two months to work on it and, I honestly don't know what I did the entire time. The past couple months went by so fast. It's all a blur.

Reading through the list I see,

- Big Ben (overdone)
- The city of London
- Queen Elizabeth (overdone)
- Duke Robert Price
- Globe Theatre

I have a feeling I want to do my paper on The Duke, and the other day I found a paper full of notes on him. I don't even remember writing them.

Here it is. I pick up the paper with the heading 'Duke Robert Price' and start re-reading it over.

- Born in Sproston Green
- Father left, lived with mother
- Put on streets: age 11
- Mother remarried to King: age 15
- Crowned Duke: age 16
- Moved to London: age 19
- Died: age 20

I don't remember writing any of this, and I don't know how I got it either. How do I know all this? And who's Robert Price?

"Why ya doin' research for?" I turn my eyes to the left and see James reading my paper over my shoulder. Then he grabs it out of my hand.

"Hey..." I try reaching for it, trying to return it to my bag. Before I'm able to, he turns to Robbie and gets his attention, but the Robbie boy looks irritated by him.

"James, just give the poor gal her papers back." Robbie rolls his eyes at his friend while I wait patiently to see if he listens or not. Something tells me he won't.

"Wait... Duke Robert Price?" I watch James start to smile as Robbie's head shoots back over to what James is holding. He rips my papers out of the red haired boys' hand and stares at it.

I watch him furrow his eyebrows as a flight attendant comes onto the speaker informing us that we may now get up and unbuckle. James sits forward.

"I'll be back." He laughs while taking off his belt and stepping over Robbie, who took this as his chance to slide into James' seat in the center.

"Is this all you know about him?" he asks while pointing to my research. I take my paper back and answer his question.

"That's all the information I have so far, yes." I let out a disgusted sound and shove my papers into my bag.

"Have you ever met him?" he asks. I look at him like he's crazy.

"No. I haven't. He was dead long before my parents even thought about having a child."

"Right. Sorry, what I meant was have you ever seen him? What he looks like, while doing research?" He turns to me and stares into my eyes. I get scared and my gaze shoots down to my phone.

"No." I say flipping through my pictures just to have something to avert my attention to. "Honestly, I don't remember doing any research. I don't know how I got that information."

Robbie's POV:

It's because I told you.

I want so desperately to show myself, make her aware of everything that really happened, but I can't not only because she won't understand, maybe not even believe me, but because she'll be afraid of me and of the demon I've become. Of the demon I am.

This is the first time I've talked to her in weeks. The last time I was this close to her, *He* was about to take her life away. I couldn't let him.

"Oh my God..." I hear her gasp and my head shoots in her direction. She is staring at the screen on her phone, studying it. Her eyebrows scrunch together, her nose crinkles in the center of her face and her mouth is agape.

Then she looks to me and her hand flies to cover her mouth, reading shock all throughout her expression. She slowly removes her hand and sets it in her lap.

"Robbie?" The word slips through the small space in her lips before she closes them into a thin line.

"What?" I watch her glance back at her phone, then to me. She went on doing this for a little while until she drops the device into her lap. She closes her eyes as her hand comes up to rest on her forehead. She looks strained.

"Are you alright?" I say while debating on whether I should grab her hand or something to comfort her. She starts shaking her head, her eyes still closed.

"I have a headache." she whispers.

"Maybe you should lie down-"

"No. I'm fine, could you just... go back over there?" she asks pointing to my original seat. I'm confused and I don't want to give James the chance to be near her again.

"Not until I make sure you're alright."

"I already told you. I'm fine." She opens her eyes and I see that she's on the verge of tears. I shake my head.

"What startled you? What caused this?" I reach down, getting ahold of her phone.

"Don't-" She tries to stop me but I've already seen what shook her up.

"That's me..."

Forget.

"Why do you have a picture of me?" I stare at the picture of the old painting that used to hang in my gallery at the palace. I was in my armor and I had just been crowned Duke.

"Can you explain that?" Carolina's shaky voice rings through my ears. I can feel her get closer, but I can't take my eyes off the photo. She must have taken that when she came to rescue me- if you want to call it that.

"Um... no, I can't." I hesitate on telling her.

"Do you remember taking this?" I ask her. She looks confused like she's trying to remember, and I can only hope.

"I don't think I took it..." she says while glancing over my shoulder.

"This photo is in your camera. No other folder. You must have taken it." She places her hand on her head again and I start getting worried. These headaches are being caused by something and if it's because of *Him* erasing her memory, I'll kill him.

"The picture. It's familiar..." She pauses and squeezes her eyes shut, as if every time she thinks about it- every time she remembers- the pain gets stronger.

"I know it hurts. Just try to remember." I grab her hand and hold the phone in front of her.

"Remember what?" She takes her hand from my hold and takes back her phone. She sets it in her lap and places her head in her hands. I can't stand seeing her in this pain.

"I'm sorry. Just stop. Stop thinking about the picture."

"How do you know I'm thinking about it?" she whispers with her eyes still shut in pain.

"Because. If you weren't, then your headache would go away." She peeks up at me through her squinted eyes. "You probably don't believe me. But just try. Tell me about your stay here in London. What'd you come for?"

"My college class." she mumbles obviously still in a lot of pain, but I know this will work. So- just for her- to make her feel better, I ask questions I already know the answers to.

"And did you come alone?"

"No. I came with my class and Professor." She looks up at me.

"And his name is?" I ask.

"Gates. Jonathan Gates." She already looks better.

"And where were you all staying?"

"In an abandoned dorm at some college. It really stank..." She lets out a small chuckle and opens her eyes fully, but she's right. It did stink.

"And what's your favorite part about London?" She takes a minute to think, and then she smiles.

"That I got to see it with the boy I love." She looks up at me, completely free of pain. I start to smile back. Maybe she does remember after all. Maybe she feels the same way about me as I do her. Maybe-

"Speak of the devil." she laughs while checking her phone. In big blinking letters it reads

1 new text message from: Rian

I felt my face drop. My whole body, sink to the floor. My heart- or at least what's left of it- stomped on. And in that moment, I knew she'd never remember me. Not without hurting herself.

As I watch how his text makes her smile and laugh quietly to herself, I realise that it's over, and I will never get her back.

She forgot about what he did to her. She forgot about the picture. She forgot about me, but I will never forget about her.

THE EASY WAY OUT.

Carolina's POV:

"There she is!" Rian exclaims cheerfully while holding his arms out waiting for me to embrace. We had just gotten off the plane and I've been looking everywhere for him. He said to wait at the exit, not the entrance.

"Hey..." I say dropping my bag by his side and making my way into his arms.

"I've got a cab waiting." he informs me.

"Wonderful." I lift myself up on the tip of my toes and press my lips against his.

"Do you guys just do that in every public area people are trying to walk through?" We hear a deep voice ask. He laughs causing me and Rian to break apart to find James standing beside us with his arms crossed and a smile on his face.

"Are you going to just stand there and watch us you perv?" Rian says rather loudly. James gets mad and looks like he's going to hit Rian, but Robbie appears and calms him down.

"James, come on. Leave them alone." I watch him place a firm hand on the hot headed boys' back as he takes a deep breath.

He lets out an angry huff and points to Rian.

"I better not run into you again." Then he turns to leave.

"Sorry." Robbie says to Rian before turning his attention to me. "I'll see you around, Carolina."

"Bye, Robbie." I lift my hand for a small wave and he does the same. Then catches up to James. I wonder if I'll ever see him again. The boy from my dream. I feel something tug on my arm and I let out a shocked gasp.

"Who was that? Huh?" Rian. He squeezes my arm harder and I let out a small whimper.

"That was your 'dream boy' wasn't it? Don't lie to me." I'm too afraid to speak, so instead I nod my head in response. He lets out an irritated sigh before pushing me away from him with great force. I almost tripped over my bag.

"Get your stuff," he pinches the bridge of his nose. "The cab's waiting."

I slowly grab my bag, and he hauls me off towards the taxi waiting outside for the two of us.

Robbie's POV:

"You dope-"

"Why'd you have to interfere, Robbie?" James kicks over a trash bin on the side of the road as we walk down the streets of Nashville.

"No matter how much I'd like to see you tear Rian apart, you can't just go around beating people up in the middle of an airport. On Saturday, one of the busiest days of the week-"

"Whatever, Robbie. I can do whatever I want. What are they gonna do to me? Throw me in jail?" he laughs.

"Maybe..."

"So what? I'll be out of there in less than a minute. I'm a demon, remember? And you are too. You need to start acting like one." He bends down to pick up a rock, then he smiles at me. "Here."

He shoves it in my hand and starts looking around.

"What do you want me to do with it?" I ask.

"Throw it. Through that glass." He points to an electronic store to my right.

"What?-"

"Just hurry before someone comes!"

"James. It's the middle of the night. Everyone's probably sleeping." I look around through the dark with him for a minute until he grabs my shoulders.

"Look. Obviously, you still have a good heart and a conscience. So, you're not going to work on your assignment." He pauses to make sure I'm listening. "But, one way or another you'll be a full demon. And soon.

"So would you like to do this the easy way," He lays one of his hands over the rock in my hand. "Or the hard way?"

I know exactly what he means.

'Do you want to do it my way, or *His* way?' is what he should've said.

Maybe this is the better option. Taking the easy way out, or in. I'm slowly losing my soul and I want to speed up the process. I'm through with trying to get her back. She's obviously better off not knowing me. She's safer. I can't handle the pain of knowing she's in pain or any kind of danger. I look at the rock and wrap it tightly in my fist. There's probably no going back. I raise my arm and chuck the rock with all my might, causing the glass to shatter.

JUST ONE NIGHT.

Carolina's POV:

I come home to a note written in my mother's handwriting laying on the marble table in the kitchen.

Carolina,

I'm sorry we're not here to welcome you home. Your father and I left town for a few days to visit your aunt. She was having another one of her breakdowns. We left the keys to the car so you can get to and from your college class as well as school. Please be careful. And no one over until we get back, I know we can trust you. We shouldn't be more than a couple days, a week tops. Aunt Kays contact information is on the fridge. We love you baby! Be good.

-Mom

After reading the letter, I place it back on the countertop and lean against the wall. I feel tears rush to my eyes as I slide down to the floor and pull my knees into my chest. They're never home anymore and with Rian acting like this lately, I'm not sure I want to be alone.

Lost in my thoughts, I almost don't notice a knock on the door. I hurry and wipe the fresh salt water from my cheek bones before dragging myself to the door.

I stop with my hand holding the door handle and take a deep breath, praying to God that it won't be Rian on the other side.

Robbie's POV:

"Watch and learn newbie." James turns and starts to fix his hair.

"Where are we?" I try to ask, but he ignores me and starts banging on the door of an unknown residence. Then he decides to answer me. "The next step is to let go."

"Let go of what?"

I'm cut off by the door being opened. It's Carolina. She has puffy red eyes and she looks exhausted, like she had been crying.

"Hey, babe. I was wondering if you wanted-"

"Are you alright?" I lean past James to make sure Carolina's okay, completely cutting him off.

"I'm fine." She wipes her eyes and looks towards the ground.

"What are you guys doing here? How do you know where I live?" she asks. I glance up at the stone building. She has a really nice house. Based on the fact that she told me her parents never get her anything new or expensive, I figured they were broke. Not just that they put all their money into their amazing house instead of their as equally amazing daughter.

"How'd you get that?" Carolina asks. I look at James and he's holding up a card that used to be attached to her suitcase. It has all her information on it. He must have ripped it off when no one was looking.

"Here..." I say grabbing it from James' hand and giving it back to her. She looks confused. "Sorry to bother you."

She nods and I turn to walk away. I hear the door shut behind me and shortly after, I hear James.

"What the hell man!"

"I'm just not ready to let go, quite yet..." I take a seat on her front porch and James takes a seat beside me.

"Why are we here?" I know I've asked already, but I feel like that wasn't a good enough explanation. James exhales and looks at me.

"Honestly, I thought since we don't really have anywhere to stay, we could well, stay here." I give him a confused look and he continues. "I know. 'How would I get her to agree when we've been nothing but rude-"

"We?" He shoots me a teasing scowl which I gladly return and he backs down. "Alright. Me. I was rude. The point is, you're not a full demon yet so you can't do this but, just trust me. She would've said yes to me.

"I figured if we stayed with her you would find closure and let go. Once and for all. Because let's face it, you're never going to achieve full demon with the thought of her lingering around. Your love for that girl is way too strong." he laughs while saying the last part more to himself than anyone.

"How would you know that?" I feel the heat rise in my cheeks, I really do like her. James starts to laugh again and I look up at him.

"It's another thing I can do. I can see what you're feeling. But lucky since I don't have a heart, I can't feel it." I nod but he continues. "You really don't know, do you?"

I feel my shoulders drop along with my head.

"What don't I know?" I ask cautiously, my voice cracking slightly. I immediately expect the worst. But before James can say another word, the chained door behind us unlocks.

We both turned around to see a very shocked Carolina slowly closing the door behind her.

"Why are you two on my steps?" she asks hesitantly. I look to James and he nod his head in her direction while rolling his eyes at me.

"Umm..." I slowly stand up and brush off my jeans. "You don't happen to know of any cheap hotels around here, do you?"

"Do you not have a place to stay?" She looks a tad bit confused. I glance towards James and he's following my previous actions of standing.

"Not really. Where we originally planned to stay suddenly became, unavailable..." I mumble loud enough for her to hear.

"We were just wondering if you knew of a place for us to stay for the night." James takes ahold of the conversation because I start getting nervous. I guess he can tell because apparently, he reads people's emotions like a book. Literally.

"Just the night?" Carolina asks me. My eyes widen and I slowly nod my head yes.

"Alright. Just one night."

Getting settled in.

Carolina's POV:

"This is the first guest room." I say stopping in front of the door. I'm not quite sure if it was a good idea, but what's done is done. Just one night, right?

"I'll take this one. Thanks." James rushes inside and slams the door. I glance to Robbie and he shrugs.

"Sorry about him." he says while rubbing the nape of his neck. James, I'm not fond of, but Robbie, I could get used to him staying. He doesn't seem to be like James at all, and the way he apologises for his friends behavior, that's what I think is sweet.

"This is your room." We stop at the room next to mine. "My room is actually right there. So if you need anything, just knock."

I watch him nod then I realise we're going to be sharing a bathroom.

"Robbie?" I catch him before he heads inside the room.

"There's a bathroom in James' room and yours, but yours is conjoined with my room." I watch a small smile form on his face as I speak. "Hope you don't mind sharing. To be honest, I'd rather share with you than 'hot shot' down there."

Robbie chuckles then apologises again for James' behavior.

"He's got a big head sometimes. Thank you though."

"It's not a problem. I'm just happy I could help." I smile as I talk.

"Goodnight!" he calls as I start down the short hall. I turn and give him one last smile before disappearing into my room.

Once inside I let out the breath I had been holding in. There's something about that boy. Robbie. The boy from my dream. He was sweet, shy, and somewhat familiar. I swear I've seen him before. Not just in my dream. Not on the plane. Not in the park.

I know him. I've met him. No matter what Rian says.

I feel my headache start to make a reappearance. Then I remember what Robbie had said about the picture. Don't think about it and it'll go away. Maybe if I don't think about Robbie, my head will stop pounding. I'm not sure why though.

I choose to take his advice. So, I change into some shorts and a tank top for bed. I fall back into my bed sheets and patiently wait for sleep to come.

TELL HER EVERYTHING.

There were two. Two of him.

The one on the left, fully clothed, arms cleared of markings and curls gone wild. On the right, tight clothes, inked skin and tamed curls.

There were two of him, neither said a word. My dream Robbie- on the left- stood there with his hands by his sides and a sweet smile on his face. The other: evil, dark, dangerous. He had his hands behind his back and a flirty, sinister side smile was playing on his face.

I was comparing them. There was nothing else to do. They wouldn't speak. Even when I asked them a question.

"Who are you? " I asked the dream Robbie. His smile dropped along with his head.

"What are you doing here? What do you want from me?" I asked the other one. This time, he let off a deep chuckle, never taking his eyes off me.

There's no way they can be the same person. They looked exactly alike, besides the fact that their clothes are different, and their hair, but their attitudes were polar opposite.

I came to the conclusion that since dream Robbie was the one I saw first, he's the original. So I turned to the other and asked him a question. Hopefully he'll answer.

"You've changed." I pointed out. "Why?"

His smile widened as he bowed his head. He stood there for a while, just staring at the ground until someone came up behind him. James.

He nudged sinister Robbie and both their gazes shot to dream Robbie. Then James chuckled. As James moved closer to dream Robbie, the other crossed his arms in front of his body and watched the entire scene.

"What are you going to do to him?" I screamed, but neither of them listened.

I watched as James grabbed dream Robbie's shoulders, dream Robbie desperately tried to get out of his grip, but couldn't for some reason. James must've been too strong. James leaned his forehead against dream Robbie's, and suddenly he was on fire.

"No! Stop!" I yelled watching as James backed away while laughing.

Dream Robbie was screaming in pain while burning on the floor, then he disappeared, and there was no trace of him or a fire.

"Oh my God." I felt tears brim in the corner of my eyes and James took notice to me.

I nearly screamed while covering my mouth at the sight of his eyes. They were black. All black.

"Get away from me!" But he just kept coming closer. Then Robbie appeared directly in front of me, eyes black as sin. Just like James.

"No..." My tears were racing down my cheeks by now. All he did was laugh. Then he grabbed onto my arms lifting me off the ground so we're the same height.

"You're next..." he whispered to me.

A groan came from deep within his throat. It sounded anything but human, and his eyes changed to fire, just as James' did, causing me to scream.

And I saw Hell...

Robbie's POV:

"Carolina! Carolina!" I'm shaking her. She just isn't waking. She's screaming and I know, this is James' doing.

"Carolina!" I yell once more. Seeing her like this makes me want to cry, but I can no longer do that.

"What are you screaming at?" James walks in wearing only his jeans.

"Robbie?" I hear a short whimper from behind me. I turn my head and see Carolina cowering beside the headboard.

I sigh as a wave of relief washes over me.

"You scared me half to death."

"Yeah right..." James lets out a disgusted noise while leaning on the door frame.

"It was just a dream, Carolina. Are you okay?" She looks from me to James a few times before shaking her head and moving to the other side of the bed.

"I'm fine." she says placing her hand on her forehead.

"Are you sure?" James says from the doorway. I look to him and he's smiling. Yes, he did this.

"Yeah." She lets out a deep breath and looks at me.

"Is it something you want to talk about?" She's just staring into my eyes, waiting for something.

"No. I'm fine. You guys go back to sleep." She stands and heads for the bathroom.

"Thanks for being there though." she whispers before closing the door.

"Anytime." James laughs while exiting her room. I follow him, closing the door behind me.

"What's wrong with you?" I ask catching up to him. "She was nice enough to share her house with us and you take advantage of it!"

He rolls his eyes and turns to me.

"I don't care." he laughs.

"Well, you should-"

"For God's sake, Robbie! You and your 'I'm still good on the inside' crap is really starting to piss me off." I stop at my door but he keeps walking.

"Look," he says getting my attention before I go inside. "When I'm working, you do not interfere. Understand?

"Good." he says while slamming his door. I didn't even agree. He must have felt how I realised I probably shouldn't refuse him. He's on a much higher level than I am, and I'm not strong yet.

I walk into the room Carolina let me stay in and pass the bathroom door. As I do, I hear quiet sobs.

I press my ear against the door, and the whimpers get louder. I thought about knocking and asking if she is alright, but she'd probably just pretend she was.

Hopefully she didn't lock my side of the door, I thought while placing my hand on the knob.

"Carolina?" I whisper while entering. When I walk in all the way, I see that she was leaning up against the shower wall with her knees pulled tightly to her chest.

When she notices me, she sniffs and starts quickly wiping her cheeks.

"I'm sorry...I was just-"

"You don't have to explain." I say while closing the door. I hop over the shower edge and take a seat beside her.

"You still don't want to talk about it?" I ask while resting my arms over my knees.

"No...um..." She looks up at me staring at me for a minute or two. Then suddenly, she changes her mind. "It just felt so real."

'That's because it was...' I think to myself.

"What was it about?" James probably used her information- like her greatest fears and her past- to get her. To scare her.

"I don't know you, but I trust you." she whispers while quickly glancing up at me then back at her exposed toes.

"I feel like I have to..." I nod even though she can't see me.

"The dream was about you and James. You both had black eyes and...I don't know. It's just stupid and I'm overreacting-"

"No, you're not." I'm debating on telling her, I really am, but decide not to. "It's alright to be afraid."

"But I'm letting this dream get to me." She looks up at me and pulls her knees in closer.

"I know this must sound crazy, and the last thing I want to do is scare you off..."

"You can tell me anything." I reach over and grab her hand. Surprisingly, she lets me.

"That's just it," She squeezes my hand and my entire forearm starts to tingle. I haven't touched her in so long. "I feel like I know you, even though I just met you yesterday."

Is she remembering?

"I've been having dreams about you..."

"Oh?" I say through a smile. She starts to shake her head.

"Not how you're thinking." She leans into my side. Hesitantly, I lift my arm and lay it over her shoulder.

"I've seen you before, before we met. I've dreamt of you like we knew each other." She starts to slowly play with my thumb, sending chills down my spine. How is she so comfortable around me? Enough to do all this.

"The dreams. They weren't dreams. They were more like a memory. Maybe." When she said a memory, my head shot over in her direction.

"A memory of when?" I ask as she places her hand on her forehead. I can tell she's getting a head rush again, but this time, it might be worth it.

"I'm not sure. Not too long ago. I still remember everything in detail, so it couldn't have been too long." She starts to explain.

"They started at the beginning of my trip to London. One of them were when we met in an abandoned, I don't know. Some kind of shop. And another one, I even lived with you in your apartment. Apartment..?-"

"7B." I answer for her. She looks up at me with confusion and shock because I was right.

"How do you-"

"Know?" I finish. She nods and I so desperately want to tell her. I open my mouth to tell the truth, but instead this is my excuse.

"Just a guess." And that's the worst excuse I could ever come up with. She looks as though she doesn't believe me, but she nods anyway.

"So, what happened in the dream tonight? " I feel her shiver underneath me. Recalling and reliving the dream James played for her must be awful. If he hurts her, I'll beat the good-for-nothing, creep.

"You said we had black eyes?" I question.

"Yeah. But at first it was you and the boy I dreamt about. Which was you, but you looked different." She gets out from under my arms and faces me, criss cross. I turn towards her sitting exactly like she is so we're facing each other.

"The other you had curls so long they dropped down into his eyes." She runs her hand through my styled hair making a few curls fall loose.

"And, his eyes were a lighter shade of blue... kind of baby blue- like, instead of ocean blue." Her hand continues to trail down the side of my cheek while admiring my features. Once she gets to the side of my mouth, she places her thumb over the crease in my cheek.

"Same dimples though." she smiles. Her hand goes down my bare chest to inspect the ink forever embedded into my skin.

"I don't think you had these." She points to the humongous, horned creature in the center of my chest. She begins sliding her finger down my abdomen. She passes over the tattoo I have of a fallen angel just under the other, and stops when she hits the top of my jeans.

"You dress differently too..." She says more to herself, even though I can hear. I feel something on my knee, so I look down. She starts picking at a loose piece of thread on my pants at the cause of the stitching coming undone. I have a giant hole in the right knee because of it, but she doesn't seem to mind, she likes messing with it.

"I just don't know how I could dream of you, then meet you...?" She shakes her head, then shakes the thought away and removes her hand from my knee.

"I just stood there comparing the two of you. Then, James walks out from behind you, and you guys were dressed almost the exact same. In all black." She says staring at the shower wall behind me; she looks terrified.

"James walked over to the other Robbie... I don't know what he did. He just grabbed him and suddenly, he was on fire." I watch as tears threaten to spill from her eyes.

"It was so real. You were right in front of me, burning. I could almost smell the ashes, the smoke and burning flesh." She scrunches her nose up and wipes the water that had escaped off her cheeks.

"Then you appeared in front of me. Not the other you, but you." I nod for her to continue.

"You had black eyes and a sinister smile on your face." She stares into my eyes, but she isn't looking at me. She was remembering what I looked like with black eyes instead of blue. She was remembering me as a demon.

"At first you towered over me, then you picked me up. You were so strong, it was like nothing to you." It's natural for a demon to be incredibly strong.

"You... you told me..." Tears start falling down her cheeks.

"It's okay." I lean forward and give her a comforting hug.

"You told me I was next, and I don't know, but just like James you set me on fire. It was like Hell." she speaks softly against my shoulder.

"Hey..." I hold her back at arm's length and wipe away the tears that had fallen. "I would never hurt you."

She's been staring at me for the longest time, then she smiles and says, "I know."

I'm happy she trusts me, but I realise James is up to something.

"We should get out of here. Besides, I think I'm sitting in a puddle." I glance down to the water seeping through my jeans. She starts to chuckle and I can't help but smile at that sound. I hadn't heard her laugh in a while.

"Come on." I stand and start to help her to her feet. "You need some rest."

"I'm not sure I could go back to sleep." She was still very shaken up and frightened.

"Alright. How about we watch a film?" I step over the shower ledge and hold my hand out for her, which she gladly takes. Once both her feet are planted on the fuzzy blue carpet, she nods.

"Good. You get it started, I'll be right back." I walk out of the bathroom, through my bedroom and to the hall. My fists clench together as I remember what she told me. Black eyes. Demon eyes. The comparison of the old me and me now. The ghost me and the demon me. How James had killed the old me representing how I had changed. How I am no longer that boy.

He tried to send a message. That I was dangerous. He's trying to pin her against me. Closure, he said. Yeah, right. He doesn't want to help me. I push his door open and find him lying on the bed.

"How's it goin', Robert?" I stand at the end of the bed watching him move his hand around in circles. Then he snaps, and his thumb catches a flame. I furrow my eyebrows and he notices.

"Cool trick, huh?" He snaps again creating an even bigger flame. The smell of smoke lingers around my nose and around the room.

"How's your girl?" he laughs, his gaze not yet looking away from the fire.

"Now that you mention it..." I take a step forward getting even more angry.

"Whoa... calm down there, Robbie." He raises his hand while sitting up.

"It's not like *I'm* the one who killed her." he smiles.

'You set me on fire... it was like Hell...' her scared voice echoing throughout my head. He made *me* do it.

"How dare you use me to scare her!" I raise my voice.

"I can do whatever I want, Robbie." he laughs while turning the fire blue, a fluorescent color.

"Can you really set people on fire like that?" I ask. He smiles at me then shrugs.

"Do you send people to Hell?"

"No." he laughs. "Only *He* can do that. But I can show them what it feels like."

He hops up off the bed and stands before me.

"So how scared was she?" He is so amused by all of this.

"She was terrified." I whisper through clenched teeth, feeling even more angry that he wants me to give him feedback. "I won't be your informant."

He starts laughing and tells me that I don't have to be.

"I was just wondering." I start to walk towards the door and he follows.

"Just give it a rest. At least for tonight." I beg him. He chuckles and shakes his head.

"I can't do that." I roll my eyes and walk back into my room, finding Carolina on the edge of my bed.

"Did you get the movie started?" I ask but she completely ignores my question.

"What did you mean by 'how dare you use me to scare her.'?" She's staring at her hands folded in her lap. She overheard.

"What are you talking about?" I watch her slowly roll her eyes.

"I heard almost everything, Robbie." I bite down on the inside of my cheek. She knows that James caused that dream. "Will you just tell me what's going on?"

I take a deep breath and sit beside her. She slowly moves over, careful not to be too close, and it almost kills me.

"You were right. Those dreams were memories. And you do know me."
I try easing the information onto her. She's already getting suspicious. I had to
tell her everything. Starting with what James is trying to do to her.

DON'T FALL ASLEEP WITH A DEMON IN THE OTHER ROOM.

What happens if a car comes?
We die.

I feel Carolina stirring from beside me indicating she has dozed off to the film we were watching. I take my eyes off the screen for a brief second to see she had rolled over onto her back, now facing the ceiling instead of the TV. She looks so peaceful, and I thank God of how understanding she was through all of this.

Earlier tonight, I had completely opened up to her. I reminded her of everything in her past that she had "forgotten". At first, she brushed it under the rug trying to forget. She said she didn't believe me. Then she got scared finally realising that what I was saying, was the truth.

But once I told her everything I knew about Rian, she understood. I told her that the reason I'm still holding on, is her. It's always been because of her, and she needs to be safe. She decided she had enough for one night and asked if I still wanted to watch a movie with her. Of course I said yes.

So, here we are about an hour- it feels like- in and she's fallen asleep next to me. If we were in her room, I'd just shut everything off and let her get some rest. That is until James tries to pull another stunt like that again.

But we're not. She set it up in the guest room I'm staying in, making it even more difficult for me to leave her be. Lord knows James won't stop, and I want her to get as much rest as she can.

I guess I'll give it until *The Notebook* is over, then I'll carry her back into her own room.

...

I lift up my head and my eyes immediately adjust to the darkness. I fell asleep. I let out a long sigh letting my head drop down to its original position on top of my folded arms.

I peek through the barrier to see Carolina still sleeping. She's laying on her back with one hand on her stomach, the other under her head for leverage. I hate to ruin this picture, but she can't sleep in here. I lift up in bed and cross my legs.

"Carolina?" I give her shoulder a shake and smile when she doesn't wake up. She must be exhausted.

"Carolina, wake up." Still no reaction, so I hop off the bed with a light chuckle and walk around to her bedside.

"Love. We have to get you to bed." This time when she doesn't move, I get a little confused. My smile drops along with my shoulders.

"Carolina?" I shake her to the side, this time with a little more force and try to pay attention to her breathing. Suddenly I realise her chest is not moving up and down, and her lips are parted slightly looking rather dull, so I begin to worry.

"Carolina!?" I lift up her hand and watch it fall back down to its place, lifeless.

"Oh my God..." I say to myself. What's wrong with her?

"Carolina, please..." I place both my hands on either side of her face and try everything to wake her. I bring my hand to her wrist to check for a pulse finding a slim one slowly restoring my hope.

I scoop her up in my arms, her limbs hanging dull in my embrace as I carry her to the bathroom. There's only one thing I can think to do before calling the police. I carefully get into the shower with her body resting in between my legs.

"Please let this work." As of now, I'm not sure who I'm talking to.

I reach for the knob turning the water on full blast. The freezing droplets rush towards us landing directly on her face. I watch her blink at the slightest, then go into a coughing fit.

"Thank God." I silently praise the beads of water as I wipe them from Carolina's face. She hasn't looked up at me yet, but at least I know she's conscious.

As I move the wet strands of hair from her face, the water continues to run. Then I see something unexplainable to the human eye. Some kind of dark mist- resembling a cloud like substance- rises up and out of Carolina, slowly leaving the bathroom through the walls. Towards James' room.

"It's okay," I whisper to Carolina when she starts to squirm, obviously in pain. "He's gone now."

Still with her eyes closed, she hugs close to my chest as my arms wrap tightly around her torso. By now, she was drenched in water. As was I, but it made him back off. Almost like it hurt him. As the cloud left, this screeching sound was heard, but they're both gone now. Makes me wonder...

I'll deal with him later. Right now, I have to make sure Carolina is safe. She lets out a small whimper, so I leave a comforting kiss on her forehead.

"It's okay. I won't let him hurt you again. You're safe..." I remove another strand of hair from her eyes and pull her closer to me as if I was the only one who could protect her. "I promise."

Good and Evil.

I've been seeing a lot more of Carolina each day, and not too long ago she admitted to me that now, I'm her only friend. I'm not sure how much I believe that. She told me she's been avoiding Rian at all cost. She broke up with him over the phone, not wanting to do it in person- afraid of how he'd react.

She called me over to talk about it and when I got there, she was in tears- scared to death. Turns out, Rian had threatened her. He told her not to act out because he'd be seeing her soon; they could talk about it then. I guess the separation was only wanted on Carolina's side. I stayed at her house that night after she had asked me to. She said, 'I only feel safe when you're around.' Though she shouldn't.

James is always following her, waiting for a chance to get to her without me interfering, but I can tell you now, that's not happening. I haven't spoken to him since Carolina kicked him out that morning after he almost killed her. We got into an argument when I shoved him, but he deserved it after everything he has done.

I actually haven't gone anywhere near the office either. Down there, ya know. I just don't know what they'd do to me knowing I'm saving a charge and having constant guidance and protection over her. That's just not how things work. I told her everything that night. Except that I'm a demon. I kind of lied about that. I told her I'm supposed to become a demon when the truth is, I already am one. I feel myself slipping away a little more each day and it terrifies me, but I'd never tell her that.

I also didn't tell her how I really feel about her. I mean, there's definitely a reason I want to protect her. The problem, I don't exactly know what that reason is. I can't even understand my own feelings. Sometimes, I honestly do wish I didn't have them. Not just the ones I have for Carolina, but in general. Giving in to *Him* and James seems like the easy decision, but I can't.

'There's a battle between good and evil and it's raging inside of me.'

Carolina gave me a list of songs to listen to a few days ago when we came upon the topic of music. That one in particular stayed with me. I seemed to remember that lyric. Quite honestly, right now I don't care what they'd do to me if they found me. I'm just going to continue to hide out and protect her.

"You've got that look again..."

"Hmm?" I snap out of my daze and look to my right.

"You were lost in thought again, Robbie. You were spacing, again." I watch Carolina as she searches through a rack of clothes. No emotion to her voice.

"Sorry. It's just... a lot's happened since-"

"I know. You don't have to explain." She grabs a dress and a couple of tops, and tells me to sit in the waiting room. After she tried them on, she modeled them for me, all of which looked gorgeous on her. She really is just too beautiful.

"Cash or credit?" I hear the employee ask.

"Credit." Carolina swipes the card as I grab her bags.

"You're all set! Have a wonderful day."

"Thank you." As we're walking towards the door Carolina tries to take her bags, but I pull them above my head and out of her reach.

"Robbie..." She groans in playful irritation.

"Nope. I'm not letting you carry these. It's the least I can do for you letting me stay at yours."

"Hey, I'm benefiting from that too. What if Rian comes over? Or even James. I need you there. To protect me." She smiles trying to sneak a bag.

"Still no." She tries to stretch, so I lift my arms higher, I'm even on my tip toes- she must have grown since I saw her last. "You'll have to do better than that. Jump froggy, jump."

She stops jumping and rolls her eyes, still with a playful smile.

"This is ridiculous. Just give me one. You're carrying like, five."

"This is nothing. I could carry more, and you being you- if I know you at all- are a shopaholic. We're far from done." I laugh at her, finally being able to bring my arms down. Man, that was a workout though. What are in these bags? Did she buy the entire store?

"Oh please, weakling..." She takes one bag in one hand and starts to take another, but I refuse.

"Weakling?" I laugh, surprising her and myself by picking her up and throwing her over my shoulder, still with bags in either hand.

"Robbie, put me down! This is not some cheesy romantic comedy." she says repeatedly banging on my shoulder blade.

"Hey, I happen to like romantic comedies-"

"Robbie!"

"I'm not putting you down until you admit, I'm the strongest boy you've ever known. Man- no, person you've ever known." I laugh at how she continues to lightly hit my back as if it'll faze me.

"Fine. Now put me down." I can tell she's getting irritated.

"Nope. Not until you say it."

"Okay, you're strong. I'd like to get down now please." She's starting to laugh. I can feel her chest vibrating through her stomach onto the very edge of my collar bone.

"What? I'm sorry, I couldn't hear you over the fact of how I'm about to bench press you, and my knees have yet to buckle once." I switch the one single bag in my right hand to my left and start to lift her by her hip to do a bench press. That is until she stops me.

"Okay okay..." She sounds extremely scared. "You, Robbie Cunningham, are the strongest person I've ever met. In fact, you're the smartest, cutest, funniest, most down to earth guy I've ever known, and I adore you."

All the laughing stops as I set her safely back on the ground and look her straight in the eyes- which are kind of widened now.

"What?" I awkwardly chuckle and she lets out a just as awkward cough.

"I... um..." As I watch her search for the words, a smile finds its way onto my face- as it always does when I'm in her presence.

"That's not what I asked, but thanks?" I chuckle as she gets all red.

"Well, I guess I can tell you now. I was waiting until we got home but," She moves a strand of hair out of her face and lets out a deep breath. "Honestly, I don't remember a thing about you. I remember of you, but that's about it."

I watch her tug me aside to sit on a bench in the middle of the mall.

"But I believe you, everything you told me. Everything you cared about enough to remember that I didn't-"

"No. No it wasn't like that. You know it wasn't, I told you. *He* erased your memory. It wasn't that you didn't care. It's that you had no choice but to forget." I remind her.

"I know. The point is, that even though I didn't "know" you, I feel like I do. This past week has been refreshing and that's enough." She smiles up at me and I can't help but do the same, but the smile quickly drops when I notice her leaning closer. My eyes widen as I watch her lips slowly open and get ready for what'll happen next.

"Carolina...?" I ask in a shuddered, nervous voice. She immediately stops and her eyes pop open. I look away from her, ashamed and she clears her throat.

"Oh." she mutters while gathering up her shopping bags.

"Carolina, wait." I sigh trying to get her to stop but she's already heading through the mall and out to the parking lot. When I finally do catch up to her she's almost at her car.

"Hey, wait a second..." I try grabbing her wrist. She flinches at first but then complies, turning to me hurt and embarrassment written all over her face.

"It's not that I didn't want to kiss you. I did. I do. It's just..." I look down at her as she patiently and fearfully awaits the rest of my reply. I take a deep breath and tell her the truth. "I don't know how."

She immediately lets out a fake, hurt, sarcastic laugh and turns back to the car door.

"Honest, Carolina! I'm telling the truth." She slams the door shut but rolls down the window to hear me out.

"I just can't remember a time..." I place my hands on the window sill and lean down to look her in the eyes- which are now brimming with tears. If she cries...

"A time when I had kissed someone. I can't remember a lot from my past life actually." She looks away from me and leans her head on the steering wheel.

She lets out a sigh of defeat and relief.

"Sometimes I forget you're a ghost." she laughs. You mean demon, my subconscious mind reminds me.

"I just don't want to mess this up."

She nods to herself and I chuckle, resting my head on my folded arms.

"I wouldn't mind having a teacher though." She peeks at me through the hair that has fallen in her face and gives me a strange look.

"What? Just because I've never kissed a girl before, doesn't mean I don't know how to flirt with one." I reply and she giggles.

"Well, I could arrange for you to get a tutor?" she comments, lifting her head up to meet my gaze fully.

"And how will I be paying for this tutor?" I chuckle and joke along with her.

"Hmm..." she pretends to think and I go into a fit of laughter.

"I believe it's a reward in itself." she whispers causing the laughter to die down a bit, but for the smile to remain.

"Are you gonna get in or what?" she says nodding to the passenger side. I smile and jog to the other car door, sliding in and buckling up.

"Let's go home, mister. We've got a lot of work to do." She winks at me and pulls out onto the road.

...

"Oh hey, by the way. Great news! We found you the perfect tutor." Carolina says sticking her key into the front door of the house.

"Oh did you?"

"Mhm." she mumbles stepping inside the extremely dark walkway to the house.

"And she's good?" I play along.

"The best there is." I let out a laugh while slipping out of my jacket as she flips on the light switch. My heart sinks when I suddenly hear a blood curdling scream come from Carolina. Before I could even turn fully around, I had a feeling I knew what was happening. My breathing hitched and I ran to Carolina holding her close inside my embrace as she lets out hysterical, scared cries.

"It's okay..." I mumble to her while rubbing down her hair. I don't dare look away from her, but I have to see what he has done now.

I glance up and I can feel my face going pale as I'm going to be sick. He's definitely gone too far. James has messed with Carolina for the last time, I guarantee it.

Thank you.

I look around the enormous mess he made. Not only had he trashed the place, he wrote a very spine tingling note to her in what I can only assume is blood, and the smell is even worse. Like there's a rotting corpse somewhere in the apartment missing a lot of blood. Carolina continues to sob uncontrollably in my hold, staining my once dry shirt with her tears.

"Hey. It's alright, love. Look, you stay here and I'll go check it out..." I start to unwind myself from her frail body when she grabs my hand.

"Please. Don't leave me." I look into her eyes and she's freaked out. There's no way she'll be able to sleep tonight. At least not under this roof.

"Okay, okay. We'll go to a hotel and call the police in the morning, alright?" I assure her, even though I'm not sure that calling the police is the best way to handle it. Police vs. demon, they'd surely lose and a lot of lives would be lost as well.

She looks up at me and nods.

"Alright." I lean down and press my lips to her forehead, slightly calming her.

"Let's get you out of here." I look around at the mess one more time before draping my arm around her waist, grabbing my jacket and pulling her close as we exit.

"What's the closest hotel?" I ask while flagging down a car for the two of us. She's too shaken up to drive, I know it.

"The Plaza. It's around the corner." She answers with sniffles in between. Soon enough we're at The Plaza and booking a room with her parents credit card. Good thing they haven't come home yet. Who knows what could have happened if they had been there.

"It's not too bad." I comment while walking into the single bed hotel room behind her.

"It'll do for tonight." She drops her over-the-shoulder bag in front of a small chair in the corner of the room.

"Thank you for bringing me here." She wipes her cheeks and starts fiddling with her thumbs.

"Of course." I slip my jacket off and take quick strides over to where she is. I place my hands over hers and guide her over to the bed to take a seat on the side. "Would you like some tea? I'm sure this hotel's got something."

I don't even wait for her response before checking every cupboard in the miniature kitchen- way too miniature if you ask me.

"No, it's fine." Her small voice causes me to stop. "Let's just go to bed."

I nod and walk over to the bedside she's on and start to help her remove her shoes. A small, weak laugh comes out of her slightly chapped lips. I furrow my eyebrows in confusion.

"I can handle this. You go get ready for bed." I lower my head as I stand, as if I were a young boy in trouble. Until she grabs my hand pulling me towards her.

"Thank you though. You sweet boy." She runs her other hand across my cheek and I start to smile. I feel her place her thumb above the spot my dimple would be and I chuckle. Then she releases me from her grasp so I could get comfortable for bed.

"I wish we had brought some clothes." She laughs while setting her tennis shoes on the ground beside the bed.

"We left in kind of a hurry." I joke.

"I know. Hey, you don't mind if I take these off, do you?" I look to her and she was unbuttoning her jeans. I hesitate at first, but the longer she waits for an answer, the more tension grows in the air.

155

"Of course not..."

She smiles and says 'good' under her breath while removing the item of clothing and setting it in a neat pile beside her shoes. I shake the image out of my head and start putting an empty sheet across the single chair. I hope this is comfy.

"What are you doing?" I hear Carolina ask from across the room. I freeze in my spot.

"Situating myself a place to sleep?" I begin to continue when she stops me again.

"No you aren't." she laughs. "There's enough room on here for the two of us. We just might have to squeeze."

"I don't know. That won't be very comfortable-"

"Anything will be more comfortable than that chair." she says.

"I meant comfortable for you." I say while setting a couple pillows down on my pallet.

"Would you stop worrying about me so much and come here?" She pats the other side of the bed and waits for me to move. I exchange looks between the pallet I've made on the chair and the comfiness of her bed for a while before she lets out a groan and gets up.

"It's not a difficult decision Duke..." She laughs at the name she called me while dragging me to the mattress. I slip off my black skinny jeans leaving me in my black Calvin Klein's and black T before sliding under the comforter with her.

"Goodnight, Robbie, and thank you again." she whispers as I turn to face her. I watch her eyelids slowly shut, a small smile playing on her lips as her whole body starts to relax.

"And thank you." I whisper placing my hand on the pillow beside our heads. She places her hand on top of mine, instantly intertwining our fingers.

"For what?" She lets out a small yawn, almost asleep.

I lean down leaving a small kiss on the knuckle of her hand as I watch her smile, drifting deeper into slumber.

"For walking into that bookstore."

THE ART OF CONTROL.

I wake up to the sound of sobbing. When I turn around, I see Carolina facing the other direction.

"Are you alright?" I ask placing a hand on her shoulder.

"Yeah... actually no. I had a really, disturbing dream. It," she pauses and turns around to face me. "Back at my house. Was that written in blood?"

She looks terrified. I don't want to tell her it was, freaking her out even more, but I don't want to lie. It looked like blood to me.

"It could've been anything." I whisper grabbing her hand in the process.

"And it was from James?" she gulps. I nod and she starts repeating the letter he left. "*He* chose you for a reason. *They* wanted you, so *He* chose you..."

Those words sound oddly familiar.

"But that's all I could see without walking into the kitchen. What do you think it means?

"Robbie?" I feel her shake my shoulder, but I can't break from my thoughts.

"I don't think that note was left for you..." I whisper remembering what James had said when we first stayed with Carolina.

'Why else would you think *He* wanted to hurry and turn you?'

He being the head of the underworld.

'You really don't know, do you?'

He was cut off when Carolina interrupted. What do I not know? Who are *They*?

"*They* wanted you, so *He* chose you...they were fighting over me." I say, sudden realisation coming to me.

"Who's they?" she asks.

"I know you feel like I protect you, but you're not safe with me." I speak the sad truth.

"Why would you say that?" She sits up abruptly and looks down at me. "I know I've asked you this before, but I have a feeling you haven't told me the complete truth. What's going on?"

"You're right. I haven't told you everything, but that's because there's a lot I'm still unaware of." I sit up and turn on the lamp on the bedside. "Carolina, listen. As much as it pains me to say this, I think it's best if you just forget about me."

I can see tears starting to form in her eyes. Not being able to watch her cry, I get up off the bed heading towards where I laid my jeans. As I start to get dressed and gather the rest of my stuff- my jacket- I hear a soft whisper coming from the bed.

"No." she says, her voice not strong enough.

"Carolina-"

"No, Robbie. You're not getting rid of me that easily." She gets up off the bed and stands directly in front of me. "I don't care if I'm in danger by knowing you. I'm in even more danger without you."

"Carolina, stop. It's not safe either way. You need to just forget. That way, if *He* comes looking for me you won't be a threat. He'll leave you alone."

"*He*? Who's *He*?" she starts to raise her voice.

"I already told you.-"

"No. What you told me was that *He* is a really bad guy who is after you. You never really explained. You can't keep running from this! Tell me who *He* is and maybe I can help you!" she screams still on the verge of tears.

"There's no way you can help. I'm trying to protect you, isn't that what you want?!" I drop my jacket back on the floor where it was.

"Not if it means losing you!" she snaps. "Just tell me who *He* is and why he's so dangerous.-"

"Fine! *He*'s my ruler!" I shout instantly hushing her.

"He's the boss..." I let out an irritated laugh while pinching the bridge of my nose.

"The ghost ruler?" she questions with a hint of sarcasm.

"No, the demon ruler! Are you happy now?!" I stare at her as she looks at me with wide eyes. "I'm half grown. And I only have a short amount of time before I'm a full one."

I watch her start to shake her head. I knew this would happen. If I had told her the truth she'd back away completely, but maybe that's for the best.

"I'm just like James! And that dream you had, is true. When we get angry, our eyes go black. We get assigned to torture innocent people for kicks! If I wanted to right now, I could tear you to pieces and wouldn't even break a sweat." I don't know what happened to me. I just started screaming, channeling all my anger that had built up from *Him*, James, Rian, Walter. All of it, is being taken out on her, and I can't stop it.

"We command fire! We control fear! We are the reason you wake up in the middle of the night sweating with tears running down that pretty little face of yours. You humans brush it under the rug exclaiming, 'It was just a dream!' " I let out a sinister laugh before continuing. "Well guess what, babe. It's not. It's all real! The dreams, the fear, the horror, the death. And no one can stop it!"

I can feel my heart racing, beating inside my chest, but it wasn't from anger any longer. I can feel the change within me as I watch Carolina slowly take a step back, but it only encourages me. A smile makes its way onto my face- and deep down I knew it wasn't right, but at that moment, the process had overtaken me. Robbie... was gone.

I slowly blink my eyes as my chest continues to rise and fall with every deep breath, and when they open again, I can feel they were in their natural state- a state that I had never been strong enough to achieve. Black.

"You wanna know what the worst part is?" I smile while taking a step towards her quivering body. She seems to be frozen, but I can't read her emotions. They're blank.

"The only person that cared about you, had just been taken away from you." I whisper while finding my speed and appearing in front of her.

"That's not true." She shakes her head.

"Oh but it is, Taylor. And I think it's about time we let you relive that dream my pal James was ever so kind to play for you." I start to pick her up by the shoulders, but she doesn't move, like it didn't faze her. She just stares at my once blue eyes.

"This isn't you..." All I could do was laugh. "You need to snap out of it!"

I blink again, my eyes changing scenery and showing her the thing that scared her most and made it real for all of us. I show her fire and her pulse quickens.

"Robert, please..."

"Don't call me that!" I throw her to the floor and she gasps.

"It's who you are!" She quickly stands up and watches me pace back and forth, palming my all of a sudden, awfully sore eyes.

"No, it's not." I breathe.

"Yes it is! Please, come back!" She's now crying and I can feel it. Not the sorrow or pity for her feelings, but the hurt emotion running through my veins making me stronger. This is what James was talking about. There's no feeling like it.

"Robert-"

"Stop calling me that!" A growl slips out from deep within my throat. "Robert died back in 1752!

"Just face it, love." My smile was back and the pain in my eyes was gone. "There is no more Robbie. And Robert is long gone. All that's left is a corrupt, sinful, immortal creature who feeds off the fear and pain of others. And if you don't like that, I'll be happy to lower Nashville's population count."

"Stop. This is not you. You are nothing like James!" She takes a step towards me. I must admit, she has guts.

"Yes I am! We are both demons! I'm just like him!"

"No you're not!-"

"Babe. Don't make this harder than it has to be." I laugh.

"Don't call me that." she snaps.

"Ooh, touchy..." I lift my hands up in a mocking tone, surrendering as I walk around her in a small circle.

"You know, I kind of like that." I whisper in her ear making sure my breath goes down her neck giving her chills.

"Babe." I repeat while squeezing the edge of her bum with my hand, noticing she's still in her knickers.

"Stop!" She swats my hand away.

"What's wrong? Don't like it when I touch you?" I laugh while purposely grasping two handfuls of her firm arse and pulling her into me.

"Stop touching me you creep!" I finally let her go and she starts to speak. "Robert wouldn't do this. Neither would the Robbie that I know."

I roll my eyes and instantly get irritated with her.

"For God's sake! How many times am I gonna have to tell you?! This is what I am! This is what I am now!" I scream letting another growl escape.

"I don't care what you are! It's who you are underneath!" she yells while coming towards me. She reaches out and grabs my hand intertwining our fingers, and I couldn't look away from them.

"And that's all that matters..." I furrow my eyebrows in confusion.

"I know that Robbie- and Robert- are in there somewhere." She places her other hand on my chest and takes another step closer. "You just have to channel them and not your anger. This is all James' doing. He's getting inside your head. This is him, not you."

I stand there, frozen at the sight before me. She unhooks our fingers and places that hand on my cheek. She slides her thumb across my bottom lip sending shivers down to my toes and that warm feeling that disappeared for a while comes rushing back.

"It's getting harder to control." I whisper finally calming down and resting my forehead on hers.

"I know..." I feel a single tear escape and land on Carolina's cheek taking weakness along with it. "But we can't let *Him* win."

Do it on my own.

James' POV:

"Can you get to him or not?!" A deep voice growled clearly getting irritated with me.

"Just give it a second..." I forced my eyes closed and felt myself leave my own body- yet somehow, I'm still here. I watched the cloud of mist I recognise to be my apparition make its way through the air.

The reason I'm here is because I was called down to speed up the process of Robbie's changing, and when I say got called down, I literally mean called down.

"That girl is a hazard! She's no good for him..."

"Actually, she's the exact opposite. She's too good for him, and that's the point. You should've just let me get rid of her when I had the chance." I said trying to focus.

"You know why we can't do that. Just hurry along." *He* instructed.

"They're gone."

"What do you mean they're gone?" I wandered through Carolina's house searching for either of them. Finding nothing, my subconscious headed for the door. Before leaving, I noticed a bunch of bags scattered across the floor. They've been here. They must have seen my surprise and ran.

"They left." I commented.

"Find out where!"

"I'm working on it." I got a bit irritated. I stopped everything for a minute including the searching through the many shopping bags on the ground and the listening to *Him* gripe, in order to just feel. I could sense where Carolina was. She was close. So I started to use that feeling that I had been given by *Him* to find her in precious situations. Because she was assigned to be my target I should be able to find Robbie. There's no way he isn't with her. Pretty soon, I could sense him as well.

"He's angry..."

"Good. Then it should be easier to change him." I wandered through some hotel's lobby and up to what I assumed they booked as their room. Then I saw them and immediately notified *Him*. I tried to stay unseen as I watched Robbie and Carolina in a heated discussion.

"What are they doing?" *He* asked.

"Talking." I heard a growl and *He* told me to interpret the conversation. "Robbie just told Carolina to forget about him."

"Maybe this will be easier than we thought."

"I'm not so sure about that. She's refusing to let him go. And I can see he doesn't want her to leave either."

"Then change his mind! Do it for him!" *His* attitude changed completely. I started to laugh at how naive Robbie was and said, "He thinks we'll leave her alone if he's out of the picture."

I heard a deep laugh as I watched the scene before me, but suddenly my breath hitched.

"He just revealed you."

"What?!" *He* growled. "Change him! Now!"

I jumped at the sudden anger and proceeded with *His* instructions. I opened my eyes and began feeding Robbie my emotions.

'You're just like me... You're eyes are black, like mine. You torture people like I do. And you enjoy it...'

I saw Robbie grow angry. His body and his soul were no longer under his control, but under mine.

'Fire, fear, even her bad dreams: It's all us Robbie...'

Pretty soon, I got him so far gone he started thinking up things by himself, and I was just there to watch the change take place.

'Call her babe...'

I laughed and a somewhat similar chuckle came out of Robbie's mouth as well. Then he listened to my instruction and called her the pet name I had come to learn she hates.

'You're changing and you enjoy it. You're in control and no one can stop you. You are *that* powerful...'

I could see how he was enjoying the power. He was just ashamed. That feeling will be gone soon enough.

"He's changing..." I reported and *He* seemed pleased with me.

"Good. I think it's time to give our spawn his eyes." *He* instructed. I watched as Robbie blinked and suddenly, black was all I could see. There wasn't a trace of blue in sight. I felt the little part of him that was left panic.

'Don't worry... it comes with the job...'

I watched him step closer to Carolina and tell her he was gone, and I was proud. I never thought he'd give up that easily, but Carolina still hasn't backed down. I could tell she's scared, but not of him, for him.

'Call her... Taylor...'

And again, he obeyed. I watched him threaten her and pick her up.

"Looks like he's ridding himself of the problem."

"On his own?" I didn't answer.

I watched her call Robbie by his full name, and he backed off a tad, "We're losing him."

"Get him back! Now, James!" *He* yelled, suddenly I could sense *Him* beside me.

'There is no more Robbie. There is no more Robert. This is what you are now...'

He repeated what I said, but she still was not convinced.

"Try a different approach!" *He* instructed. So I did my best.

'Move in on her...'

I watched Robbie get closer and suddenly, I was in control of his body. Which I've never been able to do before. I could only control someone's mind, not their entire body. Nonetheless, I made it happen. I made him get behind her, maybe squeeze her a tad; definitely taunting her.

'This is what you are...'

He repeated.

"It's not what you are, it's who you are underneath."

I heard Carolina's voice, nice and slow.

'Don't listen to her Robbie...'

But I could tell he's already calming.

"It's getting harder to control."

Robbie told her. On his own.

"No!" I fell to my knees in exhaust as the rest of me found its way back.

"You lost him, didn't you?" *He* stood before me. All I could do was stare at the floor in shame.

"It's too strong-"

"For you! Worthless..." *He* roared and started for the doors. "You want something done right, you do it yourself."

He's a lucky one.

Robbie's POV:

I now know what James meant.

'Your love for that girl is way too strong...'

It is strong. It's just the thing I need to overcome this. As long as she's around, I'll be fine. I've been so worried about protecting her, when all I needed to see is that she's protecting me. From myself.

Where is she?

I get out of bed and start to search the small hotel room.

"Carolina?" I knock on the bathroom door and suddenly hear the shower turn on.

Okay, I exhale. At first I had thought the worst. I thought she really had left despite what she had told me last night. Or rather, this morning.

I start to calm myself and walk into the other room, but the bathroom door opens so I turn to face a very shy looking Carolina wearing only a short towel to cover herself. My jaw almost drops, but I hurry and shut it before she's able to notice. I can't stop staring at the towel covered portion. She awkwardly coughs and my gaze meets hers as my cheeks instantly grow redder in color.

"Um... Do you think you could run home getting necessities?" she asks, but all I can notice is how pink her lips look. She seems sort of flushed, but it just draws more attention to her mouth.

"Robbie?"

Wow; the way my name just rolls off of her tongue. I so badly just want those lips on mine right now.

"You're scaring me, Robbie." She begins backing into the bathroom getting ready to shut the door making me realise what I was doing.

"I'm sorry." I shake the thought out of my head. "Uh, what'd you ask?"

I must seem ignorant to her. When really, I just can't stop thinking of her. I can't focus.

"If you could run home and grab us some stuff..." She seems to be being careful and cautious of me.

"Of course. You'll be okay on your own?" I ask. She nods her head pulling the towel tighter around her body causing her curves to come even more into view. What is she doing to me? Does she even know how she makes me feel.

"I'll be back before you even realise I had gone." I start to put my pants and shirt back on so I can run to the house.

"Carolina?" I turn back towards the door and she's watching me with a questioning look- one eyebrow being higher than the other.

"You know I'd never hurt you, right?" I ask shyly. "I'd do everything in my power to protect you."

A small smile starts to tug on her lips, but quickly drops along with her head. How can I prove it to her? How can I make her believe what I say is true after what's happened. Coming up with a shaky plan, I slowly make my way beside her. Her head shoots up, her beautiful eyes staring into my once again blue ones.

Considering the major height difference, I have to lean down quite a bit. She's still just watching my every move.

Soon, I form enough courage to place my lips on hers for the first time. The feeling is indescribable and I can't help but think she's perfect. The way her lips quivered at first, eventually growing comfortable with me and placing her hand on my jawline. Our lips slowly started moving in sync. This wasn't just my first kiss with Carolina; as far as I know, this was my first kiss in general.

167

I eventually back my head away from hers with a giant smile on my face. I can't seem to get it to go away.

I listen to her giggle as she runs her hand down my neck placing it on my chest.

"I'll be back." is all I can manage to say.

"I'll be here." She quickly pecks my lips and disappears behind the bathroom door. I reach up and press my fingers to my smile. I still feel the tingle of her skin lingering on my lips. Chuckling to myself, I walk out of the hotel lobby catching a car.

"Wow..." I breathe when I get settled.

"A girl?" The cab driver asks turning the corner. All I can do is nod with that same stupid smirk.

"You must be a lucky one." he laughs.

I really am.

Gone missing?

When the cab pulls up to Carolina's house, there's a cop car in the driveway.

"Thanks." I tell the driver and shut the door. There's also another car in the driveway. It must be her parents. I turn around trying to catch the cab but it's already down the road.

"Great..." I've completely changed my mind; there's no way I can go in there, and this is definitely not the way I wanted to meet her parents either. As I walk up to the door, I remember the mess James had left. The blood.

I creak the door open and the mess is still there. Books and papers are scattered all over the floor, claw marks were ripped into the wallpaper, and a vase was broken in the corner. I take a deep breath and call out through the house.

"Hello? Mrs. Taylor? Mr. Taylor?" No one answers so I walk down the main hall. The blood that was written on the wall is still there, but some yellow tape is making a border keeping anyone from entering. So I still couldn't read it fully.

"Can I help you?"

I jump and turn towards the voice that caught me leaning over the tape that specifically says do not cross. A short woman stands in front of me with her arms folded against her chest. A tissue in her hand. She looks upset with red puffy eyes; she's been crying.

"Oh, um-"

"Dear." A man comes up behind her and places his hand on her shoulder. "Who is this?"

"Sorry," I reach my hand out to his. "I'm a friend of Carolina's."

That seemed to of upset the woman even more. She turns around and buries her head in the man's chest.

"I'm sorry. I didn't-"

"It's alright." the man says still comforting the woman. "It's nothing you did."

A moment of silence goes by- with the exception of her sobbing- but is interrupted by a police officer.

"Alright, Mr. Taylor. I think we have all we need. We will send someone in to take care of the mess, and if we hear from your daughter, we'll let you know."

Carolina's father starts to thank the officer when I interrupt.

"If you don't mind me asking; what's going on?" Carolina's mother looks as though she would cry again at any second. She bows her head and answers in a hushed tone, "She's gone missing."

"We arrived an hour ago. The house was a mess. Blood was everywhere and we couldn't find Carolina. We immediately thought the worst." Her father steps in, comforting her mother once more.

"Well I can assure you, Carolina's fine." They look at me with confused expressions.

"Son, what are you talking about?" The police officer takes a step forward.

"She's been staying with me-"

"Oh thank God!" her mother says while wiping her tears.

"Why?" Her father looks angry, and I can tell he's getting defensive trying to protect Carolina, but that's also what I was doing.

"We um, went to the mall together the other day and um..." The way her dad is staring me down scares me. It's making me nervous.

"Spit it out, son." The police officer joins the conversation.

"I dropped her off," I lie. "And we came home to, well, this."

I motion around to the mess.

"She got scared so I took her with me." They all have different expressions. Her mother smiles, her father's ready to kill me and the officer is just confused.

"Why didn't you report it?" he asks.

"We were going to this morning, honest. We just woke up."

"It's almost one." her father points out.

"I sleep late." I shrug. I'm fairly sure he knows I'm lying.

"So Carolina is at your house?" the cop asks. I debate on telling them.

"Well, a hotel-"

"What is she doing at a hotel?!" her father starts raising his voice.

"What he means is..." Carolina's mother looks at me, waiting.

"Robbie." I tell her my name.

"Robbie." She smiles. "Why not at your house?"

"That's definitely not what I meant and you know it-"

"Shh. Richard." she shushes him and waits for my answer.

"Because, I don't have a house?" I say more in the form of a question.

"What do you mean?" she asks. I look at Richard and he's trying to keep his cool.

I let out a deep breath and say, "I live in London, normally. That's where I met your daughter. I came here with my friend James."

I feel myself cringe at his name. "I can't very well stay with him anymore, so I don't have a house."

"So you were staying at a hotel?" her dad asks.

"No. I only rented that room for Carolina so she'd feel safe-"

"So where were you staying?" her mom- who I still don't know the name of- asks.

"Nowhere..." The room is now filled with silence while everyone stares at me and I stare at the ground.

"Richard." I hear Carolina's mom whisper, and I peek up at them.

"We'll talk about this later. First, you're going to take us to our daughter." he says pointing at me. All I do is nod.

"I'll call someone in for clean up while you're gone." the officer says.

"Alright. Thank you." Carolina's mom replies while her dad starts dragging me to the car.

MY DAUGHTER IS BACK.

Carolina's POV:

Well, I don't have any clothes yet, so I can't exactly get dressed. I guess it doesn't really matter. Robbie's seen me in a towel this morning. Before we kissed. I didn't even know he was going for it. He looked so shy, almost frightened to do it, but that's what made it cute. I can't believe he doesn't remember how a kiss feels. I'm glad I was the one to remind him. I guess while I wait, I can tidy up the room.

I pull my towel tighter around my body hooking it on the side so it won't fall. Then I made my way over to the bed. I know they have maids and housekeeping for this kind of stuff, but I just don't like seeing a mess, and since I'm waiting around anyways, why not?

As I'm finishing up and flattening down the bed spread, I hear the beep from the key card. Oh, I forgot the body pillow. I pick it up and while placing it on the bed, I greet Robbie.

"Gee. Took you long enough. I've been sitting here in this stupid towel for an hour..." But when I turn around, I didn't see just Robbie.

"Mom? Dad? Why are you-"

"Get your stuff, Carolina. We're going home." My father picks up my dirty clothes I set on the dresser and hands them to me.

"Hurry and get dressed." he instructs.

"Why aren't you clothed?" Robbie whispers as I pass him to get to the bathroom. I could see the pink in his cheeks.

"You were supposed to bring me clothes, not my parents." I say rather loud.

"That's enough. We'll talk about this when we get home. Right now, all I'm worried about is you not being exposed." My dad stops our side conversation.

As I walk into the bathroom to change back into my old outfit, I hear my father mumbling, 'this is highly inappropriate' to either my mother or Robbie. Maybe both. The entire ride home my father has his eyes on Robbie, watching him through the mirror. Every so often, I can feel Robbie shift uncomfortably. It's making me mad. We didn't even do anything. It's not like I had ran away. It's just a friend helping another friend.

If my father really knew what was going on and how Robbie's been protecting me- in ways he never could- maybe he'd think a bit differently. Or not. Who knows. He can be really stubborn at times.

Once we pull into the drive, I rush out of the car, slamming my door and making sure that they hear it. I take a deep breath trying to calm myself down. First things first. I'm changing these gross clothes. I pick out a new pair of jeans and a shirt when I get to my bedroom. The outfit was cuter, fit better and most importantly, clean.

As I'm putting my hair up, I hear a few knocks at my door. I watch through my mirror as my mother enters my room and I can't help but roll my eyes.

"Your father wants to speak to you."

I reluctantly nod and join her downstairs where Robbie and my father sit across from each other- Robbie on the couch, my father in his chair. I walk into the room but my father's eyes never come off Robbie. Robbie awkwardly makes eye contact with me for a split second, so I send him a reassuring smile. He looks down to his hands, twiddling his thumbs, and smiling to himself. I walk over sitting next to him on the couch, and my father's expression hardens.

"Do you want to start off by telling me what you were doing in a hotel across town with a boy we don't know while we were gone? Or should we skip that and cut straight to the punishment." he says.

I raise my eyebrows at his tone and suddenly my defenses came up.

"Well, I think we should talk about what's going on instead of jumping to conclusions." I snap at my father.

"Fine. Enlighten me. Tell us what happened." he says sarcastically. I glance at Robbie, then roll my eyes.

"We went shopping and came home to a trashed house with blood on the walls. It obviously wasn't safe for us- er me- to stay here. So Robbie got us a hotel room as far away from here as possible. That's where we stayed-"

"Why were you in a towel?" my dad asks growing impatient.

"I took a shower and had no clean clothes-"

"Because heaven forbid we reuse our slightly dirty ones." he interrupts me with sarcasm. "You re-wear your shirts when your mother doesn't get around to laundry. So that's no excuse."

"It's not an excuse to walk around in only a towel in front of him," I point to Robbie. "I asked him to come here- despite the mess- and bring me back a clean outfit. Being the gentleman he is, he gladly accepted. But instead of clothes, it had to be you."

I roll my eyes at the fact that he's obviously not trusting me.

"So nothing happened?" My mother spoke for the first time causing Robbie to jump into the conversation as well.

"No, ma'am. Absolutely nothing. We just went to the hotel to get ourselves out of danger. I mean, if someone broke into your house, trashing the place and leaving a very disturbing message, I wouldn't want Carolina to be here either." He sounds like he genuinely means it, which makes me smile.

"Dad, there's nothing for you to worry about; I promise." I watch my dad lose eye contact, huffing and mumbling things under his breath. So I decide to speak up again, this time with a little more anger.

"I'm still a virgin if that's what you're wondering, dad." His eyes widen and my mother has the same reaction. Robbie uncomfortably shifts in his seat beside me, but I keep going.

"How irresponsible do you think I am? Honestly. You can't trust me? What I can't seem to understand is that you trust me enough to send me to

London with about twenty other college boys for a couple months, but you're upset that I stayed with my friend for a night?"

"Carolina, would you spare me the sob story. We trust you and you know it." he spits.

"I never said you didn't. I just don't understand your reasoning. I get your concern, but reasoning? I gave you the best reason but you still don't believe me!"

"We do, Carolina! We're just worried." my mother says while placing her hand on my dad's shoulder.

"Worried that I'll run off and get married to a boy that I've barely known for a month like you?" I watch her face fall but I can't stop. "No, mom. That's not going to happen. I think I'm smart enough to not take a chance like that, unlike some people..."

"That's enough!" My father stands up from his chair and points to the stairs. "Go to your room; I'm getting tired of your mouth!"

"Gladly!" I stomp towards the stairs. "And you might want to get used to my "mouth", you're the one who raised me to speak my mind-"

"Go! And don't come down until this smart mouth brat is gone and my daughter is back and ready to apologise!"

I look at Robbie before heading up the stairs. He had his head down staring at the floorboards. This is obviously an awkward situation for him to be in.

I slam my bedroom door and let out a long, irritated sigh. I hope my dad doesn't do anything. I wouldn't be able to forgive myself for letting that happen.

THAT WENT WELL.

Robbie's POV

"So," I look away from the stairs where Carolina had just disappeared. "What are your intentions with my daughter?"

"Oh. Nothing, sir. We're just good friends." I lie.

"Why? Is there something wrong with her?" he snaps. I feel my eyes grow wide and I think I'm starting to sweat.

"Um, no! She's lovely-"

"Then why are you just friends?"

"I- uh..."

"Richard. Leave the poor boy alone; you're obviously making it very difficult for him to answer honestly." Carolina's mom interrupts, relieving me. "He was just trying to help; isn't that right, dear?"

She looks to me and I nod, "Yes, ma'am."

"Okay. Now that that is settled, I'm Lisa, Carolina's mother. This is Richard, her father. I'm sorry if he startled you. We're just very protective over Carolina. She's our miracle child."

"Miracle child?" I ask trying not to make eye contact with her father.

"Yes. I wasn't supposed to have children, but I had Carolina." She shrugs like it's no big deal, but you can tell she's overjoyed.

"We can talk more later, but for now, is anyone hungry?" She pauses for a second and without waiting for an answer, she says, "I'll go whip something up.

"Richard?"

"Hmm?" he hums, still not taking his eyes off me.

"Would you show Robbie to his room, please?" She was about to leave when I stop her.

"My room?"

"Yes, dear. Hadn't you said you needed a place to stay?"

"Yes, but-"

"No excuses, Robbie. You'll be staying here with us until you're able to find yourself a decent place to stay. Now Richard, will you please show this young man where he'll be sleeping for the nights being." She gives him a 'do it or else' look which makes him stand to his feet, but not without a groan in reply.

"Well, are you comin' boy?"

"Oh." I quickly rise and follow him to the steps.

"This is my study." he says pointing to the bedroom where James stayed. "Don't go in there. It's off limits.

"This is Carolina's room. Don't ever go in there. It's off limits, especially to you." He pinches the bridge of his nose as we make our way to the last guest room. I guess I'll be staying in the same place I was earlier. "This is where you'll stay. There's a bathroom already inside; knock before entering. There are a couple rules..."

Oh no.

"Number one: Pick up after yourself. My wife might be nice enough to do it for you, but she is not your maid. That includes laundry, dishes and any personal belongings. Do you have any personal belongings?"

I'm afraid to speak, so I just shake my head.

"You don't?"

"No, sir." My voice comes out high pitched and cracked. I haven't really had any personal belongings since I've been a demon. The last time I had something to call my own, besides a change of clothing, is when I first met Carolina back at my flat in London.

His eyes let up somewhat on the anger and in its place I see pity, but his voice keeps the same tempo. He clears his throat and continues, "Number two:

We do things as a family. If you are staying under this roof you are a part of this family. We have dinner as a family; we go places as a family. But if you are ever going places without us, you are to let us know."

I nod but he isn't finished.

"Number three: We go to church every Sunday and Wednesday. Carolina attends a young adults group session that is held every other Wednesday. I assume you'll be attending that with her. But there is an age limit. How old are you?"

"I'm twenty, sir."

"Wonderful. You'll be amongst sixteen to twenty one year olds. Carolina has been there longer than most of the teens, so she's a big part of that group. If you have any questions, ask her. Since you said you have no belongings, we'll have to take you to get some things."

"You don't have to-"

"It's fine." He puts his hand up to silence me.

"Number four: I will not put up with any foul language or disrespectful behavior in this house. If you do not respect me and my rules, I will not hesitate to throw you out. Got it?"

I nod and he says, "Good. Get settled in, wash up, and come down for supper."

I step past him and into the room. I was about to shut the door when his foot stops it about half way.

"Rule number five: and probably the most important rule of them all; my daughter, is off limits. I don't mind you two hanging out as long as it's in a public place or area such as the mall or the living room. When you are staying under this roof, you are to have no relations with her. This is not an opportunity for easy access. As long as you two are "just friends", I don't see the problem." Just great. Constant surveillance.

"Are we clear?" His voice hardens again and when I nod, he leaves. I shut the door and finally let out the breath I had been holding in.

That went well.

Miracle child.

Carolina's POV

"Carolina! Dinner's ready!" I hear my mother call up the stairs. I don't think I'm quite ready to face my father yet. As I walk out of my room, I bump into something. Turning around, I look up at Robbie's bright blue eyes nervously staring down at me.

"Sorry." he whispers while rubbing the back of his neck.

"No. I'm sorry." We start heading down the hall. "Ya know, on behalf of my father."

He let out a nervous chuckle shoving his hands in his pockets while shrugging, "Don't be. I understand."

"I still am. It's... kind of embarrassing."

"He's just doing what he thinks is best." he replies. Then it occurs to me.

"Wait. Why are you still here?" I ask before we get to the stairs.

"Didn't you hear?" He let off a flirty smile showing his dimples. "I just moved in down the hall."

I feel a smile come to my face, "They let you stay?"

"Yeah, but I have a roommate." He playfully bumps into my side. He must be talking about the conjoined room.

179

"That must suck." I laugh.

"Not necessarily. There are good things about it." I look up at him before entering the dining room.

"And what's that?"

"The girl on the other side of the door is extremely gorgeous." I feel myself blush as we walk through the doors.

"About time you guys. Come on, it's getting cold." My mother brings the rolls to the table in between Robbie and I. I sit down across from him, honestly trying not to make eye contact after that. He called me gorgeous and it made me nervous.

"So, Robbie. You said you're from London?" My mother tries to start up a conversation, but I just can't wait until they separate from each other.

"Actually, Sproston Green. But I've lived in a few different places." We make eye contact for a brief second before I blush and look away.

"Oh? Like where?" My mother seems to find him very interesting. Really, I just think she likes that he's from a different country.

"Well, Sproston Green, Gloucester and London. That's all really." He gives me a small smile as my dad joins in the conversation.

"And what made you come here? To America?" he asks.

"Um, I was going to come and stay with James- my friend from London- but, that didn't happen." I honestly think James was a good friend to Robbie; no matter how bad of a person he was, and I think Robbie's secretly devastated that he had to choose between the only two people he had left.

"So this James," my father says getting Robbie's attention. "He's from here in Tennessee?"

"Well, no..."

"Then what? England?" My dad presses on.

"No, he's from here in the states. He's originally from Florida." Robbie's getting nervous; I can tell.

"Then why were you boys coming here?"

"Um." Robbie looks to me for help. Him and James didn't come because they lived here; they were following me.

"Um, dad. Don't you think that's enough about Robbie. What if he wants to know something about you?" I quickly look at my mother, and she speaks without question.

"Yes, dear. Robbie? Do you have any questions for us?" she asks. He smiles at me then says, "I'd like to hear more about the miracle child, if you don't mind."

Oh no. Mom told him about that. She tells everyone she can the "miracle story".

"Oh," My mother smiles at him like she's happy he asked, instead of her just telling the story on her own. "Well, we were told we couldn't have children; though that didn't stop us from trying."

She smiles at my dad for what seemed like forever. They exchange a couple glances like they were reading each other's minds, but Robbie and I just sat there awkwardly.

"They're recalling the night." I mouth to him and he cringes while sticking his tongue out.

"...and one night in particular went well creating our beautiful little miracle."

"Congratulations," Robbie speaks causing everyone's eyes to be on him. "You did a wonderful job. Carolina's brilliant."

I feel my cheeks get hot as my mom continues, "Thank you. I'm very proud."

I look to Robbie and he gives me a quick wink with that famous dimpled smirk. He seems to already be winning over my parents, and nothing's really even happened between us. Nothing except for a kiss.

"Son. Are you forgetting what we talked about upstairs?" My father raises one eyebrow staring him dead in the eye.

"No, sir." Robbie says seriously while staring at his plate.

"What did you talk about?" I ask.

"It's not of your concern." my father snaps.

"I believe it is of my concern!"

"Carolina, we just went over some rules of the house. That's all." Robbie whispers trying to calm me down.

Rules of the house. Yeah. I bet my father went up there and threatened him, but I just decide to let it go before it turns into something that gets me sent to my room and away from Robbie again.

After an hour of my father giving me the cold shoulder and Robbie a death glare, I finally get to go to my room away from the awkward atmosphere.

Once I change into something comfy, I lay down on my mattress mentally and physically exhausted.

"Carolina?" I hear a small whisper along with a few knocks coming from the bathroom door. When I get up to check it, I see Robbie on the other side.

"Thank God for conjoining rooms, huh?" He smiles while shoving his hands deep into the pockets of an old pair of my dad's grey sweats.

"Yeah." I move aside to let him in, but he just stands in the doorway.

"It's probably best that I don't come in." I nod even though that killed a part of me. My dad must have scared him quite a bit.

"Is there something you needed?" I ask leaning on the door. He leans on the door frame, copying my stance with a crooked smile.

"Not really." He crosses his arms over his bare chest, just staring at me.

"Okay. Well if you're not going to come in..." I start to close the door, but his foot blocks it. "Alright. I'll just leave it open."

I walk back to my bed and decide to write in my diary. I haven't even touched it since I left for London.

I glance back at Robbie in the doorway, and he's still watching me, smiling. I playfully roll my eyes at him and he chuckles. God only knows what thoughts are running through his head, but that doesn't stop me from wondering. I open to a new page and begin a section about Robbie. I can still feel his eyes on me, watching my every move.

"So, you're just going to watch me? Is that right?" I ask not even bothering to look up. He doesn't respond, but that's alright because I already know the answer.

"What are you writing?" I hear his voice closer than it was last time, so I look up. He came into my room, like he said he wouldn't, and was now sitting on the edge of my bed waiting for an answer to his question.

"Oh. Um..." I look down and realise I've written a lot more about him than I intended to. I just let my thoughts all spill out onto this paper.

He's standing in front of me without a shirt on again, diary. He thinks I can handle it. But I'm gonna tell you this diary, I can't. I can't stand him being right next to me and me knowing I can't touch him. But that smile. Honestly since I've met him, whenever I close my eyes, all I see are dimples, dimples, dimples. And blue eyes that sparkle... Oh diary, what's wrong with me?

"It's nothing." I close it before he gets the chance to look. He furrows his eyebrows but lets out an awkward chuckle.

"Okay," He lifts his hands up in defence. "I respect your privacy."

I smile at him, and just as I'm about to take the chance and ask him if he does want to read it, I'm interrupted by a loud, high pitched screech followed by a deep growl.

Robbie jumps up off the bed and says, "We have to leave!"

But it's too late. A cloud of smoke appears and forms into a rather tall man dressed in a black suit.

He saved me.

"You were warned!" *His* voice is deep. "This girl has gotten in the way one to many times, Robbie."

"Robbie?" My voice cracks as I look up at him. His worried blue eyes stare right back at me.

"It's alright. Just stay behind me." His voice calming me at the slightest, but it isn't enough.

"How did you find me?" he asks the man.

"How did I find you?" *He* let out a deep sarcastic laugh, then continues. "Well, it definitely wasn't that useless friend of yours."

"James?" Robbie says through clenched teeth.

"Who else?" *He* shrugs. "I came here to take care of you myself, because obviously he couldn't do a simple task such as that."

"What did you send James to do?"

"Make you forget this distracting girl. No matter what it takes." The man points to me and I feel my heart speed up.

I reach up and grab ahold of Robbie's hand. He tightens his grip when the man steps forward.

"You know what I have to do." By now, Robbie's grip on my hand is bone crushing. "She's a distraction to you. Either you let her go or I do it for you. But she has to go either way."

My breath hitches as Robbie speaks, "You won't hurt her!"

"Then option number one?" The man cocks one eyebrow and Robbie starts shaking his head.

The man's smirk falls and he grows angry.

"I'm through babying you. Choose!" *He* growls, but Robbie stays silent.

"Fine. You won't come willingly, I'll make you come." *He* takes a step forward staring at me.

Robbie notices and steps in front of me, "You won't touch her!"

The man flings his hand to the side, and Robbie goes flying away from me crashing into the wall. I let out a scream and cover my mouth at the sight of Robbie. He's holding the back of his head trying to get to his feet, but clearly failing. My attention turns back to the man who is pretty close to me by now. I back up until I hit my dresser.

"Stop!" Robbie yells gathering both our attentions. He had somehow found the strength to get to his feet. "I'll go willingly. Just leave her alone. Please."

I look forward and the tall man is shaking his head.

"You don't get it, Robbie. This is exactly what I'm talking about. Distraction.

"You need to let me do this. You had the option. I realised, as long as she's here a piece of your heart will always belong to her. And we can't have that."

"Carolina?!" I hear my dad's voice from the other side of my bedroom door, but I'm afraid to speak. "Open the door!"

"We're busy..." The man yells back.

"Who is that? Is that Robbie?! I swear if you hurt her..." I watch a smile grow on his face at my dad's words.

"This is perfect. They'll think Robbie here is responsible." *He* laughs.

"Say goodbye..." *He* says starting to squeeze his hand closed causing me to grow drowsy, my body getting limp and weak as it has once before.

"No!" I watch as Robbie jumps in front of me, pushing the man's arm down knocking both him and the man in the black suit to the floor in a struggle. I cover my ears as my parents continue to bang on the door and Robbie stands to his feet in front of me, the man rising to his feet again as well.

"You don't want to do this, Robbie." Robbie grows angrier than I've ever got the chance to see and rushes at the man, who is unfortunately quicker than him. Robbie almost loses his footing, but when he regains his balance, *He* slashes his hand- that now had giant claws that had burst through his nail beds- across Robbie making him fall to the floor with a deep cut down his abdomen. I scream falling to his side, kneeling to make sure he's okay only to see that he isn't moving. He isn't bleeding either, which is something that I find strange. Do demons not bleed?

"See, this is the kind of disaster I wanted to avoid! This is what happens when love-"

He doesn't get to finish his sentence before he disappears. I wonder why he would leave in the middle of a sentence and what the rest of that sentence was, but none of that mattered right now. I look down at Robbie and pull his head into my lap. I feel as the tears roll down my cheeks and suddenly, the door bursts open.

"Carolina, are you okay? What happened?" My mother trails in behind my father. When they see Robbie, their eyes widen and their mouths drop.

I let out a few sobs then whisper, "He saved me."

Guardian Angel.

How could he be so stupid. So ignorant. My stupid, brave, ignorant, generous... Robbie. I continue to cry into his shoulder, one of my hands are tightly wound in his curls, the other clutching his now cold hand.

"You're so stupid..." I mumble lifting up and staring at his blank face. I lightly trace over the curve of his bottom lip trying to remember how they felt over mine. I didn't get to tell him... anything. I realise my parents still hadn't said anything. I don't even bother wiping off my tears before looking up to them.

"Mom?" But she doesn't move. Neither does my father. Both frozen.

"Don't worry. They won't remember." I hear a small voice coming from the corner of the room. I watch as a boy with brown hair and blue green eyes comes into view. He's wearing a white suit jacket covering his maroon T shirt paired with dark blue jeans, and he is beautiful. I almost can't keep my eyes off of him. He's glowing.

"Thank you." he interrupts my thought process with a chuckle. "It's my light."

I furrow my eyebrows still clutching onto Robbie's lifeless hand.

"I probably can't explain good enough but I can give it a shot." he laughs but I'm speechless, not to mention heart broken. Who is this guy? And why is he acting like everything's okay when it's clearly not?

"But it is, Carolina. Or it will be." he comments.

"How are you-"

"Doing that?" I nod and look to Robbie, a new set of tears forming.

"Well," He leans down next to me and Robbie's limp body. "It's kind of a long story so I'll let Robbie explain it to you."

Tears start overflowing at his words. How is he going to? I watch him place a hand over Robbie's cut.

"First, I'm William, Robbie's second guardian. His first one is earth bound. At the moment." I watch as a bright light came out of his palm and connect to Robbie's chest.

"Second, I can tell what you're feeling. Therefore, I can tell what you're thinking." The light grows even brighter but it doesn't stop William from finishing his story. It doesn't seem to faze him as much as it does me.

"I was watching the entire scene." He glances up at me then back down at Robbie's abdomen. "You really love him, don't you? I can feel it."

Love? Robbie? I'm not sure I'm quite ready to use a word with as much meaning as that one.

"Don't worry. I feel the same emotion coming from him." he smirks.

I want so bad to smile, but I can't. Not in this situation.

"Hmm..." William takes his hands off Robbie, placing them in his lap.

"What is it? What's wrong?" I run my hands through Robbie's curls as William speaks.

"He's worse than I thought." I watch him stand just to bend back over and grab Robbie's hands.

"What do you mean?" I stand up with him and he instructs, "I need you to stand back."

"What are you going to do with him?" My voice is croaky and almost dried tears stain my cheeks.

"I have to take him with me, but don't worry." He glances up at me with a reassuring smile. "You'll see him again."

And with that, they were gone and my parents were back.

"Honey, are you alright? We heard crying." my mother speaks, obviously not remembering. I stare blankly at the wall behind them not caring to answer her.

Alright? I'm honestly far from it.

MADELINE.

It seems as though everyone that Robbie was an acquaintance to has forgotten about him. Just like in London when he was taken to Gloucester. He was in serious trouble then. You can't blame me for being worried. I can't focus on anything. I'm pretty sure my project is going to be a complete disaster. I can't even read my title without breaking down. There's no way I'll be able to finish it.

Why did he have to jump in front of me? What was he thinking? Yeah, he was trying to keep me safe but he should have thought about how I would feel without him. If he had really cared about how I felt, he wouldn't have left me here alone.

I can't seem to wrap my head around the fact that he might die.

'He's worse than I thought...'

William. Who is William? Besides Robbie's second guardian. How do demons even have one guardian, let alone two. Robbie was brave. Stupid, but brave.

"Dear?" I look up at the sound of my mother's voice.

"There's someone here to see you." She moves aside and in walks a girl with curly brown locks and blue eyes. The same shade as Robbie's.

She stands awkwardly in front of my dresser with her hands folded in front of her.

"I'll leave you two alone." I watch my mother leave and once the door is closed, the girl begins to speak.

"Hi. I'm Madeline." She holds out her hand, but all I do is stare at it. I still don't recognise her, but she looks a little too much like him. As she awkwardly pulls her freshly manicured hand back, she purses her lips into a thin line causing two permanent dimples to come into play.

"I'm sorry. Who are you?" my voice cracks. I hadn't spoke in almost a week. Everything's just been too draining. Definitely not worth my energy.

"My name is Madeline. Professor Gates suggested me to your parents about tutoring since you're unable to attend class." She gives me a short smile showing those dimples that are the exact replica of Robbie's. In the same spot and everything.

"May I?" She points to the edge of my bed, so I nod. She gives me another friendly smile and starts unpacking her bag.

"You haven't really missed anything too important." she laughs.

"What have we been doing?" I whisper. She seems a bit too excited that she's the only one I've been able to talk to, but it's not her that I choose to talk to. It's Robbie, and the resemblance is uncanny. I know I can't pretend she's him but somehow, it comforts me.

"Well," she smiles and hands me a piece of paper. "It turns out the trip to London we took wasn't all that productive."

"How so?" I glance up from the hand out and find her smiling at me. I give her a confused look and she shakes her head.

"I'm sorry... um, Professor Gates said we gathered information easily but none of us finished our projects, which is, according to him 'not protocol'."

I laugh at her imitation of him and she smiles, kind of proudly. That's when mine drops, along with my head. I feel a hand on my knee, so I look up.

"It's okay to laugh." She sends me a sweet side smile. The kind Robbie used to give me when I would be worried or nervous. I don't think he'd want me to fall into depression, and that's what I'm doing. Willingly. Robbie risked his own life so that I could continue to live mine, and this is how I choose to live?

I smile at her and place my hand on hers. She mirrors my smile and takes out another sheet of paper.

"Gates wanted me to give you this." I look down at it as she tells me what he said. "He's giving us all a couple more days. But since you've been out for a week, your time's a bit limited."

"How limited?" I ask while setting down the worksheet explaining the project.

"Wednesday."

I close my eyes and pinch the bridge of my nose, "It's Tuesday."

"I know. Which is why I'm going to help you. I finished mine the other day and I know how he wants it set up." I smile at her offer and she asks what it is I chose to research.

"Robbie-" My throat starts to close up so I cough. "Duke Robert Price."

"Nice topic." she smiles. "Let's get started."

FREEDOM.

I've finally finished my project. Of course I didn't mention anything too personal about my "research" on Robbie, but I did tell her everything I knew. With the exception of the small things I've noticed like how his eyes sparkle when he laughs causing the corners of his eyes and his nose to crinkle. Or when he got angry, mostly at James, his fists would ball and veins would become visible in his neck. Any normal, sane person would find it to be scary, but I thought it was cute.

It's been a few days since I turned in my project. Well, I shouldn't say I. Madeline dropped it off. I'm still on bedrest. My parents were even so shocked about my "breakdown" they called a therapist. She visits every Wednesday and Friday, but the only things I tell her are short answers to the questions she asks.

How are you feeling today? Fine.

Feeling any better? Sure.

Have anything you want or need to talk about? Nope.

It's the same every session. I can't necessarily tell her everything. She'd think I'm loony. Send me to mental home. The thought that bothers me most, besides 'Is Robbie Okay' is why can I remember? Last time Robbie was taken away, no one remembered him. This time, I do. I remember him. So my question is, why now? Why me?

193

On the bright side, I'm talking to Madeline a lot more. We've become great friends. Every once in a while she'll come over bearing junk food and movies, and we'll sit around and talk about how class is going, or how I'm feeling. She even mentioned Rian a few times, and how he looks miserable when he thinks no one's watching or how he keeps his act up when someone looks his way. It's kind of funny. I've also found out he's dating this blonde chick from one of his other classes. Stephanie? I'm not sure, but the point is he's moved on, so. Not like I care anymore.

Something really awful happened the other day. My mother was helping me pick up some of my room, make it a little more cozy since I'm stuck in here, and while I wasn't paying attention she found my journal. I stopped her before she could read any of the good stuff, such as the Robbie stuff, but she did find out a couple of things. That there's a boy, his name was Robbie and I'm extremely shaken up about it. She's even got the feeling that he's the reason for my "breakdown". It's actually called depression, and yes, he's the reason for it. Congratulations Mom. You've finally paid enough attention to your daughter to notice something's going on in her life.

I unplug the drain and sit there in the tub watching as the water swirls down until it all vanishes.

"Done, sweety?" I hear my mom enter the single bathroom in my room, the one connecting me to the room Robbie stayed in. The one he held me in while I cried my eyes out the night he first stayed. "I'm going to leave these towels right here. Take your time, dry off and meet me and your father down stairs. We have something we want to talk to you about."

I wait for both doors to shut- the one for my bathroom and my bedroom door. Then I slowly bring my knees to my chest, burying my head in my arms and I let out a few silent sobs. Every time I take a shower- the only alone time I get- my mother tells me to take my time and that I'm not to be bothered. Most people enjoy their shower time. It's supposed to be a peaceful period to think about the days to come or to sing your heart out, but all I seem to do is cry.

I finally get out and finish up. I head down the stairs to the dining room and at the table sat my parents and, surprisingly, my therapist, Dr. Slone.

"There's my girl!" my dad sings standing up to kiss me on the top of my head.

"Come sit down Carolina. We have some good news." my mother says while patting the chair beside her, across from doc.

Once I'm settled, dad sits back down and mom starts explaining what's going on.

"Darling. Your father and I have decided that maybe it's time you finally went out-"

"Really?" I sit forward in my seat, almost ready to jog out the door right now.

"Yes, honey. Dr. Slone has shared with us that she feels it's best you get out." My father holds out the keys to the car, dropping them into my hands. "She thinks you're ready."

STRONGER.

"So we're on for Friday?"

"Of course."

"And you're sure you're ready for something as big as the cinema reopening?"

I let out a deep breath while doodling in my journal. The one where I write about Robbie.

"My parents are sure. And so is Dr. Slone."

"Your psychiatrist?" Madeline asks.

"Yep. She thinks I've improved a lot over the past few weeks. Or at least that's what she says." I roll my eyes at the thought.

"You don't agree?"

"Not with her reasoning."

"Why do you say that?" I take another deep breath and say, "Because the only real answer I gave her was a simple one word answer. Doesn't make sense."

"Hmm... Well, maybe it's not the answers you gave her it's the physical responses she's going by."

I let out an obvious annoyed groan.

"Since when did you become a licensed psychiatrist?" I ask with sarcasm while tracing over my heart for the fifth time.

I hear her chuckle and say, "Whatever. Be ready by six-"

"Do you mind if I drive? I just got the privilege to drive the car back and I wanna go for a test run."

"Sure." she laughs. "Pick me up at six."

I nod even though she can't see me.

"Oh, and Taylor?"

My heart almost drops at the name, but she doesn't give me any time to respond.

"Don't be late."

I fake a laugh and hang up. I switch my gaze away from my cell and back to the page that consist of Robbie's name, little heart sketches and a small combination of words I read in his journal the second night I stayed with him. Yet, it never really meant anything to me until now.

Sometimes you have to get away to come back stronger.

...

"Some people just shouldn't have their license... " I say while jogging across the street to the cinema.

"Happy you got your license back now?" Madeline laughs.

"It's people like that that make me wish I never had it in the first place."

We're about to enter the theater when Madeline pulls me back and takes me in the other direction.

"What are you doing?" I ask as she keeps dragging me up some stairs. Considering this is the reopening, I haven't seen it since they remodeled the entire building so I don't know where we're going.

"Madeline. I don't think we're supposed to be up here."

"Don't worry." is all she says before she finally lets go of me. She leads me up into an old projection booth overlooking an old theater room. They must not have redone everything. This area still looks like it hasn't been used in a while.

I turn around to ask Madeline why we're here, and she's not by the door where I last saw her. I start glancing around the small dark space in search for her.

In the very corner of the room, I see the silhouette of a tall figure, but I don't think it's her.

"Excuse me?" I take cautious steps towards the man until he stops what he's doing, straightens his back and starts to turn.

It wasn't Madeline, but it was a head full of brown curls, dimpled cheeks and a pair of blue eyes staring back at me.

It definitely wasn't Madeline. But it was Robbie.

I'VE ALWAYS LIKED THIS SKIRT.

"Oh my God." I place my hand over my mouth to try and stop my sobs, but it was no use. I start to break down, and he just stands there. He watches me with his hands shoved in his pockets as I cry.

"Carolina-"

"Stop." I squeak out through my tears. I can't take anymore of this.

"Whatever you have to say, you can tell me after you hold me." I say as I rush into his embrace.

I start to let out even more uncontrolled sobs when I don't feel his arms around me the way I should have. I finally pull away and look up to his eyes hoping for an answer, but I get nothing because he refuses to make eye contact.

We stand in silence for a while until he sticks his hands back into his pockets and clears his throat.

"Carolina," That's all he can get out. He stands there with his mouth open waiting for the words to come out. We both were, but they never did.

He takes a deep breath and closes it before trailing his eyes up and down my body. His eyebrows furrow as he tilts his head and walks towards me; all the while my heart is beating faster by the second.

"I've always liked this skirt." he whispers while grasping the fabric of the floral skirt he had personally picked out for me a while ago.

"I miss you." I whisper, hoping to get some sort of reaction from him.

He drops the edge of my skirt and takes a couple steps back; his hands back in his pockets, his stare now on the ground.

"I know." he barely whispers.

"Then why'd you leave?"

"To heal." he shrugs.

"For so long?"

"It was the only way for both you and I to be safe." He kicks an old film on the floor causing it to roll. We both watch it as it settles in a clutter of tapes in the corner and I ask, "Are you alright?"

His head shoots up towards me and a smile forms on his face.

"Thanks to you, I am."

"Me? How-"

"There's a lot you don't know. Hell, there's an awful lot I still don't know." He stops to chuckle inwardly. "Can we go someplace? To talk?"

My mind is still a little clouded by the fact he's actually standing before me again, and he's okay. I take a deep breath as Robbie stands patiently awaiting my answer with that stupid smirk I missed so much.

"Sure." I breathe out and he looks almost relieved. "Want to go to my house? I'm pretty sure my parents are home, but it should be fine-"

"No. I've got somewhere I want to show you." He holds out his hand to me and I must have stared at it a little too long. Robbie chuckles reaching for my wrist. He places both my hands on his chest, holding me close.

"You feel that?" he asks. I furrow my eyebrows as he continues. "You act as if I'm not real. Like I'll vanish in a split second. But I won't, Carolina.

"You feel this?" He presses his hand on top of mine over his own heart. I feel the heart beat beneath my fingers and run my hands down his abdomen, smiling when his breathing hitched the further down I got.

I stop just above where his shirt would end and pants would start, smiling to myself.

"Are you here for good?" I look up hopefully at him, but his eyes tell me I'm not going to like the answer.

"Carolina," He takes a deep breath and grabs my hands. "I'm dead. Remember? I died back in 1752. I'll never return back to earth."

I feel tears form in my eyes. He notices and pulls me in for a hug.

"Please don't cry. There's nothing more I'd want to do than stay here with you forever. It just doesn't happen like that.-"

I interrupt his little speech by pushing him back. A look of shock and worry cover his face.

"Why not though? You've been here before! This is the fourth time!" I plant my face in my hands as they muffle my sobs and hide my ugly red cheeks. I back to a wall and slide down continually crying, and only pausing when I feel his body heat next to me. He wraps his arm around me cooing 'shh, it's okay' in my ear.

"I don't get it," I say through sobs. "Why can't you come back? I need you."

"There are different rules now." He rubs my hair down as I lean my head on his chest, his chin on my head.

"Rule changes again?" He laughs as I sniff and says, "No. I've changed. Again."

I look up to him and ask, "What do you mean?"

All he does is smile.

"Come with me." He stands, helping me to my feet. "I wanna show you something."

ENOUGH.

"Where are we?-"

"Keep your eyes closed." he says placing a hand on my shoulder.

"Why?-"

"Shh. Keep your voice down too." he laughs.

I whisper an apology before getting that shushed by him as well.

"Robbie-"

"We're almost there. Be patient." he says. I can almost hear his smirk. He knows I'm not a very patient person.

"Alright." He uncovers my eyes, and before me I see a large pond filled with ducks, rose bud bushes lining the sidewalks, park benches at every corner turn off, but no one was in sight. Which is odd.

"I used to come here with William all the time." I watch him pick up a pebble and skim it across the water causing the ducks to scatter. William... the name rang a bell. His guardian angel.

When I look back up at him, he looks a little sorrowful, so I decide to leave the William topic alone.

"Where exactly is here?" I ask instead.

He exhales and says, "A place that is only mine."

I watch him stare out in awe at the remarkable beauty.

"Is that why the place is deserted?"

"Pretty much." He skips another rock.

"I don't understand." I say more to myself.

"You won't for a while, but I'll try my best to explain." He smiles down at me before taking my hand and leading me down a path towards an old broken down school house. He offers me a seat on the only swing, a small rusty block of wood held by some string. It doesn't seem safe, but Robbie wouldn't put me in any kind of danger, intentionally.

"What did you mean back in the cinema about being changed?" He begins slowly pushing me on the swing, strands of my hair blocking the view of the pond.

"I'm no longer a demon." he says with joy laced in his voice.

"Then what are you?"

He waits a few seconds, takes a deep breath and ignores the question asking, "What would you consider cheating?"

I furrow my eyebrows, instantly becoming confused.

"Well, what do you mean by cheating?" I ask as I watch him walk around the swing and take a seat before me as my ride comes to a stop.

"Cheating in general. You know," He pauses to look towards the pond. "Cheating on your girlfriend, cheating on a test, cheating death."

My eyes shoot to him, but he's still lost in thought staring out at the water.

"Robbie." I move out of the swing and take a seat next to him on the grass. I reach for his hand and he tightens it around my fingers.

He turns to me, smiles and asks, "Carolina. Do you believe in God and angels and all that?"

"Yeah, I guess I do."

He just simply nods. This isn't like him. Where's the Robbie I know? The cheeky heartbreaker that's never even kissed a girl, the complete dork with unfunny knock knock jokes, the incredibly happy boy I fell in love with?

"You are one, you know." He turns to look at me again, the expression of awe still on his face.

"I'm what?" I ask.

"An angel." He tucks a strand of hair behind my ear, letting his fingers linger a little too long on my cheek. "My angel, my guardian angel."

"I thought William was your guardian angel?" His hand drops from my face and his smile falters a bit.

"He is... was." He takes a deep breath. "I had two. William and you."

I must have gotten the most confused look on my face. That must be what William meant by, 'I'm Robbie's *second* guardian angel.'

"I'm the other..." I state and his smile fully comes back.

"Yes, well. You can't really have an angel when you are one yourself."

"Robbie. Are you telling me you're-" He interrupts me with the nod of his head.

"I'm so happy for you." I wrap my arms around him. His grip on my waist was unremovable.

"Thank you." He pulls away and gestures to everything around me. "And this is my home."

"Is it like heaven?" I ask.

"Sort of. It's hard to explain." He puts on that cute thinking face he used to make all the time while reading Shakespeare. The one where he pinches his bottom lip between his pointer and thumb.

"Let's put it this way," he pivots to be sitting directly in front of me. "Every angel when they receive their wings, they get their own heaven. It can be anywhere, look like anything, have anyone in it."

"And this is yours?"

"This is mine." he repeats.

"You said you can have anyone?" He nods.

"Then where's Gasmine? Or your mom?"

"I created this section all by imagination using inspiration from park I used to go to in my youth. Usually, the sections are a replica of happy places in your memory. A home, a childhood hangout-"

"You came up with this all on your own?" I question. He nods once again.

"I use this place to think, mainly. No one is allowed here but me." I feel a smile appear on my face after that. I feel special. He brought me.

"You're not even supposed to be up here. I just figured since I'm the only one allowed here, it'd be safe." he laughs.

"Is it against the rules." I joke.

"Oh yeah. Big time."

After the laughter dies down, we sit in silence just watching the ducks.

"What did you mean by William and I used to come here?"

"William had been in my life since, I don't know. I've just always known him. When I figured out he was my guardian angel, it all made sense. He's been watching out for me my entire life. And even after that." he laughs.

"He's the only other person I brought here besides you.

"How'd you like Madeline?" he asks at random.

"How did you-"

"I sent her." I watch him get a proud smile on his face, as a confused one made its way onto mine.

"Am I going to have to explain everything to you?" he groans. I playfully punch his arm as he laughs.

"I'm kidding." He grabs my hand and says, "When William took me, he made it perfectly clear I couldn't see you again. So I kind of begged him to at least let me be with you somehow. So I sent Madeline."

"So Madeline's not real?" I ask.

"No. She's as real as you are. She's just a little bit closer to her wings than you are." I furrow my eyebrows.

"Closer?" I ask. His eyes get a little wider as he purses his lips, then smiles.

"I think I've said too much." he laughs.

"Well, you have to tell me now."

"Actually, I don't." He stands to his feet, dusting off his blue jeans and red checkered button up. Man I've missed this attire of his.

"But you should." I stand with him.

He starts to smile at me, so I say, "Please. You can't leave me hangin' like this."

He smiles even wider and cocks up one eyebrow.

"Alright, but you have to close your eyes first."

I roll my eyes right before I close them.

"I don't see how closing my eyes helps any, Robbie." I hear some rustling then fast footsteps. I open my eyes to see him taking off.

"Robbie!" I start after the laughing moron ahead of me, but he's too fast. I stop with my hands on my knees catching my breath.

"Robbie!" I call for him, but I get no answer. After I catch my breath, I continue walking through the park. Eventually, all the trees and grass start to fade out into nothing and all I see is white. All I'm surrounded by is nothing.

"Robbie?" I start getting scared.

"So," I jump at the sound of his voice. "I see you've reached the edge of my room."

I turn around to see where he's at, but he's not there.

"Turn back around, love."

I did as I was told and he stands there with a smug smile on his face.

"How did you-" He interrupts me with a shrug.

"I just kinda can." he smiles.

"Where are we now?"

"At the edge of my imagination room." I smile as he continues. "I usually like to keep this space open. Extra room, ya know?"

Still not really understanding any of this, I nod until he starts laughing.

"What?" I ask.

"Watch."

I watch, focusing on Robbie until something starts happening behind him. My mouth falls to the ground as I watch a ginormous tree grow out of nowhere behind him.

"Would you like an apple?" He holds out his hand making a branch grow in our direction. He plucks a golden apple from it and hands it to me.

"Yellow. Your favorite."

I smile and take the apple.

When I glance back up, the tree is gone and Robbie is looking around the open space.

"What else can you do?" I ask in a quiet voice.

He chuckles not looking at me once and says, "Anything!"

"I can make this into anything I want." I watch as furniture starts forming and appearing, turning into an old styled kitchen. "My third most favorite place in the world."

I laugh at the enchanting atmosphere, then realise the kitchen was the kitchen from his apartment.

"Or maybe my second?" he says as the room changes, forming book shelves and old red couches.

"The bookstore?"

"The first place we met." he smiles.

"What's your first favorite?" I ask.

"My first?" He puts on his thinking face. Then smiles, "It looks something like this."

I watch as the old bookshelves turn into an old dresser, the couch is now a queen sized bed and Robbie has this smirk on his face that I can't quite describe.

I was about to ask where, but he interrupts.

"Wait for it." I listen and take another glance. Something about the light cream walls and carpeting is familiar. That's when it clicked; it was my bedroom.

"Robbie." He starts chuckling to himself, then jumps onto my bed.

"You should get a waterbed." he suggests.

I walk over and take the seat next to him.

"If you can make this place anything you want, make a waterbed."

"Oh yeah."

I start to laugh and adjust to lay beside him when the bed changes. I topple over with his body weight being sunk towards the middle.

"I always hated water beds." I laugh as his body crushes mine.

"Sorry," he says lifting onto his elbows above me. "Want me to change it back?"

I look up at him, his rather long curls hanging into his eyes as the blue sparkled- probably at our position.

"No. I kinda like this proximity..."

One side of his mouth twitches upward as he bit on his lower lip to try and hide the smile. I laugh as he tucks a strand of my hair behind my ear.

"I miss you." he says letting out a deep breath.

"I'm right here."

He brings his head down meeting my lips with his. That same peppermint aroma that I usually smell when we're close is now even stronger; I can taste it.

All too quickly, he pulls away but his touch lingers.

"You've gotten better." I say as he smiles down at me. "Not bad for a boy that's never been kissed before."

He cracks up and sits on the bed beside me. It was until then I realise my bed is now back to normal.

"Okay. Let's get to the real reason why I brought you here." he says turning to face me.

"How's your project going?" I furrow my eyebrows, a little confused. "It is about me, isn't it?"

"Yeah, but-"

"So. What did you write about me?" I sit up beside him and say, "It's a secret."

He puts on a pouty face and starts to beg.

"No, Robbie." I say through my laughter. "You just have to wait."

"For what?" he asks. I shrug and he rolls his eyes.

"Am I gonna have to get on my knees?" he says leaning.

"Stop you weirdo." I laugh while pulling him up by his collar.

"I'm not telling you because it's personal."

"Yes, but it involves me." I laugh and say, "Fine. I wrote about how ignorant you act and how almost everything goes over your head."

I pause to see his reaction but he is just listening intently.

"And how strong you are. Mentally. Emotionally. How kind you are and how safe you make me feel. How you're so giving and that once you set your mind to something, you stick to it. How focused you can be. How you listen to your heart. You ignore ridicule and care for everyone as if they were blood." I grab his hand and start playing with his fingers.

"I wrote about how beautiful you are. How I can't stand not being near you. It's literally become impossible for me to do anything without the thought of you or without picturing you in my mind. It's almost as if I don't do anything without asking myself, 'What would Robbie think?' and I can't take it." I feel him wrap his arms around me and wipe my cheeks. I must be crying. I didn't even notice.

"You're a bad liar..." he chuckles lowly and shifts. I look up at him and I see his damp, red eyes.

"You're right," I wipe my eyes with the back of my hand. "That's not what I wrote about, but that doesn't mean it's any less true."

I rest with my head on his chest, still messing with the rings on his fingers. I feel him press a kiss to my temple and say, "We don't have much longer until I have to get you back."

"What if I don't want to go back?" I say causing a deep chuckle to outbreak from underneath me.

"You have to, love. It's not my call." He starts to play with a strand of my hair. "But if it was, you know what I'd pick?"

"For me to stay here forever?"

"If that's what you want." He sends me a simple smile.

I thought for a minute. It is, but then again it isn't. It's not about where I am. It's about being with him. Wherever he is, I want to be. I want to be with him.

"I'm sorry, Carolina-" I glance up and he looks like he's going to tell me something bad, and I already knew what it was.

"Don't." I cut him off from telling me what I already know. That being that I can't stay. "Don't say it, I already know."

"I'm sorry..."

"Stop saying that too." I say pulling back. "Saying sorry is just a form of pity."

I look up into his eyes seeing two emotions clear as day: pity and longing.

"I don't want your pity. I want you." He closes his eyes and runs his hand over his face.

"Carolina," he stressfully groans.

"You don't feel the same, do you?" I ask catching him off guard. His hands fall to his lap and he almost looks angry.

"Of course I do, Carolina. You just have to be patient, no matter how difficult it is for you." I almost crack a smile but decide against it, and when he sees I don't, his smile falters.

"Listen Carolina," he says. As he moves closer towards me, he grabs my chin with his thumb and forefinger tilting my head to be closer to him.

"I don't care what happens along the way as long as in the end, we're together. And I know we will be."

"How?" I ask in a whisper.

He smiles and says, "Because when you get your wings, nothing will keep us apart."

He leans in pressing his lips to mine while my hands get tangled in his mess of curls. He lowers me to the cushion and pins me down by holding my sides. I feel him roll his hips against mine and at the same time, a moan escapes his lips vibrating onto mine.

"Robbie..." I mumble making him pull away breathing hard, his eyes no longer sad but clouded with lust.

"How much longer do we have until I have to leave?"

"We have a few minutes." he smirks.

"How many minutes?" He moves a strand of my hair and his eyes scan down my chest to our pressed together hips.

"Enough." Then his lips were on mine again, and it felt as though they were meant to be there.

I PROMISE.

"We'll see each other again. I promise."

He continues to repeat that sentence over and over again before he eventually says goodbye. I feel him tighten his arms around my bare waist and start planting kisses on the back of my neck.

I giggle and he asks, "Why are you so quiet, love?"

"Just thinkin'." I take a deep breath and intertwine my fingers with his.

"What about?" he hums against my shoulder continuing his attack with his lips.

"Nothing. And everything..." I exhale.

"Sounds confusing." I laugh and feel his head rest against mine, a few of his curls tickling my cheek.

"Just a little."

"Anything I can help with?" he asks.

"Maybe," I think about his offer, then decide to ask, "Who is *Him*? Or was *Him*?"

I feel Robbie's muscles tense and his grip got secure and protective.

"Just someone trying to keep me away from you." he whispers, his voice laced with venom towards *Him*.

"Why?"

"It doesn't matter why. All that matters is he's gone now and I have you." he says kissing my ear, then laying his head back down.

"Then you're not going to tell me?" I feel a puff of air hit my face as he takes a deep breath.

"I was supposed to be an angel. I was in line for my wings, like you and Madeline." I nod and he continues.

"William was my guardian angel, you already know that much, but a guardian angel is not just an angel who's a guardian over you. They're a guardian over a soon to be angel, if you understand?"

I nod once again.

"Let's just say *He* interfered and took me, trying to force me to become a demon because that's what *He* does. *He* takes people who have no one, the perfect body for a demon. Someone who has no one or no reason to say no, but I refused anyway. So *He* made a deal with me.

"*He* told me that if I could find someone who knows me and cares enough about me to give me a reason, he'd let me go. Of course he had to be a cheater and change me into a ghost so I couldn't be able to feel and see if I was close or not. So *They* sent you, to save me."

"Who's *They*?" I ask.

"Up there," he says tilting my head towards the ceiling. "William and the others, I suppose."

"Oh."

"Yeah," he says returning his hand to my stomach. "You were, as cheesy as it sounds, made for me."

I giggle and glance at him. He's staring down at me in awe with that dimpled smile.

"It was getting too serious, I guess, and we were getting too close so *He* captured me."

I watch his smile disappear as he goes through the bad memories again.

"*He* tried punishing me by taking me back to my previous life, as if I hadn't escaped or died."

I bring my hand up to caress his cheek as he gives me a sad smile for the gesture. I give him a reassuring smile as he takes my hand and continues.

"When you came to save me, *He* caught us trying to escape and gave me a choice. Your life or mine." By now my eyes are filled with tears and Robbie's grip on my hand is unbreakable.

"Of course I chose yours. *He* wiped your memory and took my soul, binding a contract for me to become a demon. That was until I found you again." He pauses to wipe my cheek and pull me closer into his chest.

"I left and stayed with you. *He* got enraged and sent for me. I guess when he saw you were willing to give your life for mine he just, disappeared." I feel Robbie shrug his shoulders and take a deep breath.

"Too much for him, huh?"

He laughs and says, "Evidently. I think it broke the contract, but I'm not entirely certain."

I lean on my elbows and look into his eyes. I grab a hold of his curls and pull him on top of me.

When our lips detach, he's smiling and there's no doubt I am too.

"I love you, Robbie." I whisper against his lips as he hovers above me. His smile grows and he closes his eyes.

"You have no idea how long I've been waiting to hear you say those three words."

I rub my thumb over his bottom lip, picturing how it would feel if he said it back, and then his lips moved, but me being in my daydream, I heard nothing.

I furrow my eyebrows and he brings his face to mine once more.

"I'm in love with you, Carolina."

Final.

We'll see each other again. He promised. I just have to be patient. Stay calm and be patient.

After he dropped me off at home, in my real room, he kissed me once more and repeated his promise, and that was goodbye, for now.

I returned to school the next day. Surprisingly, everyone was glad to see me, but it was mostly Madeline. Now that I know who she is, we've become inseparable. I even met her guardian angel, Chris. She never stops speaking of him. I think someone has a little crush.

I no longer see Dr. Slone. Unless you consider Madeline or my journal special help, I'm in the clear.

My parents gave in on all the technology and bought me a laptop and upgraded my phone. My dad even has a cell phone now. It's quite funny watching him mess with it. The other night he was texting a colleague from work and all I could hear from the kitchen was ooh and ahh that's nifty.

But, all's well and I have never been more at peace knowing who I am, what I'm here for and what's waiting for me. A life with Robbie.

"Carolina?" I look up from my journal towards the front of the room. "Are you ready?"

I nod to Professor Gates and stand gathering my papers.

I take my place in front of the room as he whispers, "Good to have you back, Carolina."

He pats my shoulder, causing me to smile. I look out to the class full of students and in the clutter of young adults, my eyes connect with a pair of blue ones with a head full of curls. She smiles showing her dimples and gives me a thumbs up, and in that moment, I swear I saw Robbie.

I take a deep breath, ridding myself of any nerves and begin.

"Duke Robert Price was a noble man..."

Made in the USA
Monee, IL
06 September 2019